MURDER ON THE SANTA SPECIAL

By the same author:

The British Hearse and the British Funeral, Book Guild Publishing, 2011

Sherlock Holmes: The Missing Earl and Other New Adventures, Book Guild Publishing, 2012

Sherlock Holmes: A Case at Christmas, Book Guild Publishing, 2013

Sherlock Holmes: The Russian Connection and Other New Adventures, Book Guild Publishing, 2013

MURDER ON THE
SANTA SPECIAL

A TRADITIONAL ENGLISH COUNTRY
VILLAGE WHODUNNIT

N. M. Scott

Book Guild Publishing
Sussex, England

First published in Great Britain in 2014 by
The Book Guild Ltd
The Werks
45 Church Road
Hove, BN3 2BE

Typesetting in Garamond by
Keyboard Services, Luton, Bedfordshire

Printed and bound in Great Britain by
CPI Group (UK) Ltd, Croydon, CR0 4YY

A catalogue record for this book is available from
The British Library

ISBN 978 1 909716 12 4

For Mum

Acknowledgements

Special thanks, as always, to all the team at Book Guild Publishing; also to Gail Woodcock, Dot and Amanda.

1

A meeting was taking place. Members of the committee were seated on canvas, tubular steel chairs round a trestle table in a dusty ante room crammed chock-a-block with props and trunks of theatrical clothes, just off the side of the stage at Bramley Village Hall. Outside, where everybody had been but ten minutes earlier, a sunny, lovely spring morning was in progress. On the gravel were parked Brigadier Eames' old silver-grey Bentley with its dusty hub caps, and a few other cars and a moped belonging to members.

In the hedgerow, great tits and sparrows darted among the foliage and there was, beyond the modern rectory, the distant murmur of the dual carriageway. Preening itself atop of the pitched tiles above the hall's main doors was a crow.

With mossy, lichen-stained, corrugated iron roof, pebble-dashed prefabricated walls, and window frames and doors in need of a lick of paint after a long winter, the village hall was nothing remarkable. In fact, similar recreational buildings can be seen in quiet English villages all around the country.

The agenda being discussed at the morning's meeting was equally familiar and perhaps predictable in the current financial climate. The chairman, Brigadier Eames, himself a lifelong resident of Bramley, shuffled through the papers of the agenda and addressed the committee in measured tones.

'The thorny issue of potholes and road mending aside, I have to relate sadly that, despite our petitions and attempts to raise public awareness, the cottage hospital faces closure in the next six months. The Health Authority has made it clear there will be no reprieve. As the committee will already know from our last general meeting, the Church of England primary school that has been on the brink of dissolution for some time looks set to shut its doors for good by the end of the year.'

'The pub by the village duck pond, The Lion, is boarded up,' sighed Mrs Evans. 'I drove round by there the other day. The Grieveses tried to make a go of it – the real ale venture and the seafood platters, Sunday lunches and the children's play area – but they've gone, had enough.'

'Pubs are a different matter,' said Mr Baxter. 'The Green Man along by the station has always maintained supremacy and been the more popular watering hole. They have loud music with those "heavy metal" nights every Friday and Saturday which attracts young people – but Bramley Primary School closing, the cottage hospital with its outpatients and maternity care – now that will hit the village hard.'

'Leather-jacketed hooligans, tarty girls who screech obscenities at the drop of a hat, overspill trash from the town,' muttered the brigadier. 'I must also mention the Bramley Cross and Brocklehurst Preserved Steam Railway.' (Brigadier Eames was Chairman of the Preservation Committee.) 'We still have that blasted bridge repair to contend with. If we could just extend the line to Fenley we might attract more visitor numbers and generate more income. Thirty thousand pounds is the builders' estimate for strengthening and repairing such a structure. I ask you, army engineers could fix it in a week. Just a lot of bricks and mortar!'

'A bridge too far,' Cheryl Bleasdale wryly pointed out, snatching another chocolate digestive from the plate.

'There's the summer Steam Open Day event and the Santa Specials later in the year, of course, and we can hopefully attract larger visitor numbers than last year. Cheryl, what's the latest on Mrs Maggs?'

'The Post Office shop is bound to shut in December, if no one else will take it on. The writing's on the wall. There's been no real interest – so far. The prices are rather steep. It's a vicious circle. Once the country bus service stopped running through Bramley and Brocklehurst villages, Mrs Maggs thought she would take advantage of the elderly and people without cars or available transport and hike the prices up. Anyone using the store is now confronted by ridiculous prices – £1.45 for a tin of sardines that cost forty pence in the supermarket, £2 for a can of oxtail soup, £2 for a loaf of Hovis, £5.95 for a pack of loo rolls. The woman's gone mad. And of course everyone's been put off going in there.'

'Online shopping the answer?' asked Mr Baxter, lighting his aluminium pipe.

'Come off it!' remarked Cheryl. 'Most of the old dears round here find operating a remote control for a DVD player more than enough new technology to handle in one lifetime.'

'Now to the final item on the agenda,' said Brigadier Eames, bringing everyone to order. 'Pass me that last biscuit if you will, Hugh. The problem of unfilled potholes rears its ugly head yet again. Our vicar took a tumble and his bicycle came a cropper because of the state of the road along Beeching Lane, and he wants something done about it. Ah, wait a mo', we have a paragraph at the end of the last page relating to what at one time was the asylum for the mentally impaired. The Birchpark Institution, which of course has lain unoccupied and virtually derelict for a number of years, since the late seventies in fact. All that land and the Health Authority failed to find a buyer.'

'Until now, that is,' said Mr Baxter, puffing away on his Falcon pipe. 'Don't tell me – it is to be magically morphed into luxury apartments or converted by a hotel group.'

'Neither,' replied the brigadier. 'We are informed Birchpark is to become a private residence, planning permission granted. Well, that's a turn up for the books.'

'Who would possibly have the money to take on such an immense and costly project? Those vast asylum buildings will need gutting,' stated Mrs Evans.

'Well, there's plenty of land, it's secluded, there's a lake, woodland. Yes, I can see the sense. Of course if you have plenty of dosh there's no problem. Perhaps whoever it is will decide to knock it all down and start from scratch,' Brigadier Eames suggested.

'No, it's listed,' Cheryl pointed out. 'The Victorian structure will have to remain standing.'

'Good luck, that's what I say. Jolly good luck! Because anyone who's prepared to take that lot on is going to need it.'

2

'A village in decline – how can that be? It's absolutely beautiful,' said a striking young brunette wearing a fashionable jacket, jeans and boots, laying her cello case on its side in the hall. 'Mrs Clagg, my sister and I walked round the village only early this morning. The little railway line, the aged church, and thatched cottages – she loves it. I too love it.'

'That may be,' replied the landlady sourly. 'You be purely visitors, my dear. For us locals the blessed buses don't run any more into town, and if you haven't got a car you're stuck. Soon be no doctor for miles. There's been no police since Sergeant Briggs left, and they sold the little cob house with its blue lamp.'

'But your rural Post Office store, that quaint Hansel and Gretel house with the pitched roof and cockerel weather vane.'

'Closing. Mrs Maggs has had more than enough – and we of her. The prices have got so steep – £1.45 for a tin of sardines in brine – ridiculous! Forced to pay £3 for a paltry sliver of mature Cheddar from her freezer, the milk's gone up as well. Oh, she's over eighty now, too old to change. Any'ow, is your papa in Moscow pleased to be spending a fortune on his daughters' little holiday in England?'

'Holiday!' Yelena, the younger sister laughed as she bounced through the front door, playfully poking her tongue out at Mrs Clagg and hanging her music satchel over the peg on the hall stand. 'Dame Moira is a tough cookie. Boot camp more like! But seriously, we *have* been allowed time off from the Moscow Conservatoire to come over here to take part in the "International Young Musician of the Year" competition. Dame Moira, who is of course a retired top concert performer, one of the greatest pianists of her day, works us very hard.'

'Well, me and Stan think both you and Svetlana sing and play lovely. You'll have our vote, that's for sure, my dears.'

The landlady fussed over her charges and sent them bustling upstairs, watching the pretty and vivacious teenagers ascend the staircase.

'Just a shame there's no buses and you have to spend so much on the taxi each morning.'

'I saw the little engine towing a carriage along by the hedge,' shouted down Svetlana from the bathroom. 'Like something out of a children's fairy tale book.'

'Lor', how that preserved railway needs funding,' bellowed Mrs Clagg, busying herself in the kitchen preparing the tea things. 'They wants to extend the line, see! To Fenley – but there's a darn bridge that needs rebuilding. That and laying more track will cost an arm and a leg accordin' to my Stan, who as you girls know, is a volunteer. Table's laid, you little imps get down here. I couldn't get any of that fancy pickled herring you talked of. Sardine sandwiches will have to do.'

3

The next morning Dame Moira took her talented pupil to task, insisting she played a passage of Beethoven's Piano Concerto No 1 with more élan, while her husband, himself a top-rated cellist, taught Svetlana in the next room. The home they shared was a modern, glass-sided, eco-friendly house etched into the hillside with magnificent views of the Downs, including the winding railway line where the occasional little engine hauling a carriage and a guard's van could be seen puffing its way towards Brocklehurst before entering a section of tunnel.

During their coffee break, Dame Moira took Yelena over to the sunny window seat and together they gazed across the impressive green landscape into the far distance.

'You can see the tower of that Saxon church I was telling you about, and the steeply pitched roof of the Victorian asylum just over the hill, Yelena. Fairly isolated, it cared for the mentally impaired. There is a recorded case of a most exquisite creature, a beautiful girl who, alas, knocked her head on the tiller of a sailing boat one holiday and suffered irreparable brain damage. From the moment of her injury she lost all memory of her past life and her personality. She had to be led around the wards like a becalmed child, no idea of her worth or fabulous looks. The asylum also housed many children with Down's Syndrome – you've heard of it?'

'Of course,' replied Yelena, sipping her coffee, fascinated by the story of the lost girl.

'Well, in those days, before medical care as we know it today, so many of these poor babes, often born out of wedlock, were locked up, only to spend the rest of their lives incarcerated in an asylum, not knowing the outside world or venturing beyond the gates – from cradle to grave in fact.'

'Do you think they suffered?'

'Not particularly. I mean, they knew no different, did they? And they were fed, cared for, kept warm under one roof, the wards and grounds being their common neighbourhood, other patients for company, never lonely in the modern sense. No, I don't think they suffered, but what I really wanted to tell you, Yelena, is that I read in the local paper that after decades of standing derelict and empty, the asylum is apparently to be converted into a private residence. I think the Health Authority tried to find a use for the place when it closed in the late seventies but its location, being so far from any town and in the middle of nowhere, put off the usual hoteliers and building speculators.'

'Until now.'

'That appears to be the case, my dear. Building permits have been granted and I hear they're already halfway through the project to make the place fit for human habitation. So the old Victorian asylum shall have a use at last.'

'It makes perfect sense. Presumably there's a lot of land attached. Someone has their sights set on making it a home.'

'Someone with money, darling, lots and lots of it. A mobile phone tycoon? An internet entrepreneur, an online fashion magnate?' Dame Moira sighed and poured out more coffee from the pot and said in almost a conspiratorial whisper, 'It will take millions to make the place habitable – fix the slates, the plumbing, the drains. The sheer vastness of such an enterprise beggars belief.'

'You will have a new neighbour soon,' said the girl, resuming her place at the Steinway piano and practising a dainty scale, while her tutor continued to stare out of the plate glass window at the lonely slate roof of the old asylum known as Birchpark.

'Yes, Yelena, that would appear to be the case. Please turn to the Mozart, could you? We'll practise the second movement of K467, No. 21 in C Major.'

4

Mr Clagg ate his lunch of ham salad and a strawberry yogurt at the kitchen table while his wife, the landlady, smoked a cigarette and did the crossword. Wild birds, blue and great tits, a chaffinch and a sparrow were busily hopping about, clinging to the wire mesh of the bird feeder suspended outside the window. The tap-tapping of tiny beaks and light notes of birdsong audible on a day of little breeze that was sparkly sunny and warm.

'That damn bridge be causing the trouble,' admitted Stan, spooning up the last of his yogurt. 'Thirty thousand pound – where are we to find that sort of money? If Southern would allow us to do the job ourselves – why, our maintenance crew of volunteers could re-cement a few bricks and stick in a couple of joists for a quarter of the costs. We could prepare the track bed, lay the sleepers and rails and be on our way. It's all down to blessed regulations. You can't do this, you can't do that. That and spiralling estimates that seem to change every week. If bloody British Rail hadn't lifted the tracks all those years ago and allowed the infrastructure to decline, including that bridge, we would not be where we are today.'

'Begging money from the banks, or the Lottery fund.'

'We could attract twice the annual visitors if we could just expand the line a further three miles to Fenley. T'would be good for us volunteers and good for the village. I reckon the management need to be a bit more pushy, take out another bank loan or summat.'

'That's nonsense, you silly fat oaf. Look, Stan, in the present financial climate, banks are under the cosh, loans to small businesses are few and far between, let alone a tiny, privately run branch line railway like ours, that's just getting on its feet. Anyway, Steam Open Day's not so far off, and there's the Santa Specials in December. You've only just completed restoring the ticket hall and parcels office. You'll have to be patient, let the bloomin' bridge slide for now. Be content with the line you've got.'

'Well,' her husband sighed, 'we've got to get the loco shed roof fixed, and get those restored carriages we're working on under proper shelter. At least that should be affordable. And our engine driver instruction days are proving popular.' Stan twisted round on his chair and gave the window pane a sharp rap with his knuckles. The birds paid little heed, continuing to trill and peck greedily at the seeds on offer, fluttering aggressively between the wire feeder and half of coconut shell filled with suet mixture.

'You seen it yet?' he asked absently, getting up and putting his plate and cutlery in the bowl of washing suds in the sink.

'It? Seen what? I don't know what "it" refers to, do I?' The landlady glanced up from the crossword, stubbing her cigarette in the Charringtons ash tray she had bought from the Oxfam shop for thirty pence.

'Bright red, latest model BMW XL SUV touring around the village, tinted windows, stopped outside the Post Office shop when I cycled past. Couldn't see anybody and no one appeared to get out.'

'Bloody townies, I expect, looking to buy a weekend place, something to convert.'

5

Edie Blenchley first spotted the helicopter when she was out visiting her friend Miss Parrish in Mouse Lane. The rotors were awfully loud as it made its approach very low over the rooftops. At first she had assumed it was the county air ambulance or a police helicopter attending an incident on the main road – but it had circled round and torn off across the Downs, where she was amazed to watch the helicopter hover for a bit before making an alarming descent and disappearing behind the hill, the distant clatter of the rotors still audible, seeming to become louder and quieter alternately, before the noise ceased altogether and peace and quiet once more reigned over Bramley village.

'No,' she recalled, telling Miss Parrish over a cup of Earl Grey, 'it was not navy blue and yellow, neither was it white with chequered stripes. It was bright red, shiny and gleaming like one of those Tri-ang toys of yore.'

'Well, the fire brigade don't own one – at least not in our county. No Edie, the helicopter you saw must have been privately owned. You're certain it was not a motorized hang glider, my dear?'

'Definitely not!' she insisted to Miss Parrish. 'Not one of those airborne lawnmowers. This was a very splendid looking red helicopter and it came down to the right of the church. But the sun was very dazzling, of course.'

'That'll be the Birchpark asylum, or the "Estate" as it's now being called on local TV news. Oh yes, the weekend

Gazette was full of pictures showing how the gardens are being re-landscaped and the lake's been drained and a new garage complex is being built. Whoever's up there knows what they're doing alright.'

Upon returning to her pretty red brick house, Edie Blenchley poured a sustaining glass of Sanatogen tonic wine, switched on the mid-morning news, and began preparing a snack in the kitchen when she became aware of a raucous and annoying vibration setting her teeth on edge and making the window rattle. She peered skywards in time to see a low-flying aircraft soar across the rooftops, the noise being tremendous, and did manage to identify the underbelly, gleaming riveted metal and black skids of the very same helicopter she had seen earlier disappearing over the Downs.

The television news was blaring from the sitting room. She paused from filling her roll with Parma ham and lashings of Colman's mustard to listen.

The Russian oligarch, the billionaire who owns a four-hundred-foot long vessel, the £50 million super-yacht 'Clara', insisted he would be keeping on his Belgravia flat and offices, but a move to the country was a delightful prospect, and one he had been planning for some time. Now we move to the football – Jackie!

6

Brigadier Eames sat at the same oak desk used by countless stationmasters over the years since the line's inception, the platform office restored to its original 1950s British Rail green and cream colour scheme and wood finish, meticulously recreated with timetable board and wall clock by weekend volunteers. Items of railway memorabilia – oil lamps and framed sepia prints of the old branch operating in its heyday, when it would have joined the main line – were proudly displayed on shelves round the room.

Tugging at his walrus moustache, the brigadier carefully considered the letter before him, at first with profound scepticism – not a fax nor a text, mind you, but an actual handwritten letter, which he noted had been posted from the Mayfair district of London, addressed to the Chairman of the Management Committee of the Bramley Cross and Brocklehurst Preserved Steam Railway.

Chairman,
I have read with interest your modest brochure of coming events and note the summer Steam Open Day, along with the popular classic car demonstration. I have recently acquired for an outrageous sum Stalin's special armoured train, comprising three coaches and a magnificent locomotive, that has seen extensive service in Siberia. If you perchance have room on your sidings, might this train be of interest to enthusiasts, a means of attracting

14

the paying public and raising both funds for and awareness of the Bramley Cross and Brocklehurst private venture? The infernal bridge repairs you mention, the line extension to Fenley, and the travails of stubborn bureaucracy you hint at in your monthly newsletter that prevent the railway's expansion are a necessary evil but can be dealt with and overcome. Believe me, citizen, I have myself much bitter experience of this problem and know my way round it.

Let me know through my Mayfair offices a suitable hour for the flat-loader trucks carrying Stalin's armoured train to arrive at the station yard, so the train can be transferred onto the sidings in good time for the steam event – at no expense to yourselves, of course.

I am sir,
Yours obligingly
Oleg Petrovich

The chairman's scepticism all of a sudden left him, a feeling akin to euphoria filling his heart, and he straightaway began composing a return letter. This evidently knowledgeable and refined Russian benefactor was just the sort of person he could do business with – a future relationship that should be nurtured. The generous offer of Stalin's – of all people! – special armoured train could prove a sensation, the ensuing press coverage on local radio and television, articles in the weekend *Gazette*. Why, it was just what the line needed, the going rate for hiring 'The Flying Scotsman' or 'The Earl of Fife' let alone the famous 'Mallard', were prohibitive. Stalin's armoured train parked along sidings by the loco shed with easy access from the goods yard was far superior a draw than any Flying Scotsman.

7

'They're building an extension,' said an excitable Mrs Clagg, placing a striped bowl of muesli before Svetlana and presenting Yelena with her usual apple and crispbread.

'An extension to what?' enquired Svetlana, politely stifling a yawn.

'The Post Office store. Mrs Maggs has been bought out and the new owners are making a mini supermarket of the place. I've never in my life seen such quality produce at the Post Office store. Gutted over the weekend, completely refurbished – check-out, new counter service area, white beluga caviar on sale, fresh farm produce, cans labelled Chekov's this and Chekov's that – microwave meals!'

'Chekov's is a popular Russian brand. The stores at home, like Lidl, price-cut everything, buying it in from all over Europe. There's a Chekov's round the corner from the Conservatoire where my sister and I are students, Mrs Clagg.'

'I am astonished, perfectly bemused how this cheap brand can turn up in a quaint English village store,' said Yelena snootily.

'The point is, my dears, the Post Office store survives. Those of us without cars still have a convenience store to go to. Who cares what nationality the brands are, you can't be too choosy, and as for your quaint little Hansel and Gretel Post Office store, they're not going to demolish it, just build an extension out back. The new people, the

16

man and wife, are very nice. Mrs Maggs got paid a tidy sum for the business, apparently.'

'Well, the prices will be fairer,' said Stan Clagg, coming in to the kitchen, hitching up his boiler suit and putting on his greasy cap as he prepared to leave for the preserved railway to coal up one of the locomotives. '£1.50 for a tin of sardines was daylight robbery.' He snatched his Tupperware box containing his lunchtime rolls. 'Brigadier Eames mentioned we've an important meeting on Sunday. Perhaps management have found a way forward with the bridge problem. All the volunteers and members are invited. A suitable loan agreement with the banks, perhaps.'

'The funds just ain't there any more, Stan. The current membership is three hundred souls, fifty of whom are active and help on the line, the railway cannot afford to go into debt. I told you before – the proposed route to Fenley is a pipe dream, wishful thinking, a bridge too far.'

'Be seeing you!' Svetlana, on hearing the loud beep-beep of Dave's taxi outside the front gate, got up from the breakfast table and dashed into the hall to collect her bulky cello case, swiftly followed by Yelena, who grabbed her music satchel and bounded for the front door.

8

The sleek red Bell executive helicopter rose from behind the hill and swept across the Downs, flying low across the roofs and chimney pots of Bramley. A huge landscaping project was being carried out over at the old asylum grounds, now known locally as Birchpark Estate.

A hubbub of building materials, heavy plant hire such as bulldozers and diggers and a Volvo mining truck with enormous chunky tyres, along with specialist workmen, had started to converge on the site, approachable only from a once little used side turning off the dual carriageway. A rural lane that ran through woods dark and gloomy from the overhanging tree canopy, it rose steeply up to the gates of the old asylum.

Low-loaders with flashing yellow hazard lamps delivered the convoys of plant machinery, crawling along the dual carriageway before turning off and freeing up the long line of traffic. The road surface of Birchpark Lane was churned up because of the frequent cumbersome vehicles using it as a thoroughfare.

Edie Blenchley had the misfortune to be caught behind one of these long vehicles when she was returning from shopping at Tesco's in the town centre. The trailer was carrying what seemed to her at least like a giant Tonka toy, a yellow truck with gigantic, thickly-treaded tyres secured by straps and chains to the low-loader. Her tiny Ford Fiesta was stuck behind the big trailer for three miles before it turned off up that concealed lane.

Edie recalled riding her Honda moped up there when she was at college and pausing to reconnoitre, wandering along by the asylum wall, staring beyond the gates at the old Victorian buildings. The slate roofs and tall chimney stacks, the square, grey building in the grounds, which she eventually found out was the mortuary where the brains of deceased inmates were removed for examination and bottling and labelling. Empty and neglected since the late seventies, when attitudes changed and day-care centres and modern accommodation allowed patients to be released into the community. Times had changed regarding health care for the mentally impaired. It was no longer deemed necessary to lock them up in wards. Asylums all over the country closed down, shut their doors for good, and now one of them, Birchpark, was to become a rich oligarch's home, the lands and estate to do with as he pleased.

The news that the Post Office store was to be saved and had been taken over by new people and prices slashed had been communicated to her by mobile texting while she was lunching at John Lewis. This was extremely welcome news for the life of the village, but another ongoing and equally significant fact was that the Russian oligarch's entourage of secretaries and business associates who accompanied him everywhere around the globe would be sending their children to Bramley Primary School, a slate roofed, grey stone Victorian schoolhouse and playground along Larch Lane, and that an investment of funds and a makeover to the classrooms, cloakrooms and toilets was promised.

'What does it all mean for the village?' she wondered, winding down the side window as the low-loader turned off and she could put her foot down at last as the road ahead became clear.

9

The cab of the chubby green and black pannier tank engine – it being the beginning of June – was sweltering hot. While young Pete Sturgis heaped lumps of coal into the furnace, Stan leant out of the cab and kept his eye on the rails, one hand wrapped in a rag kept on the regulator. The footplate rattled and squeaked as the locomotive passed through a cutting and entered the sooty mouth of the tunnel, giving a blast of whistle. Half a minute later Stan and Pete were facing the glare of bright summer sunshine. The day was hot and sunny and the single carriage they were coupled to was full of passengers who had been enjoying an excursion up the line as far as Badgers Halt. Suddenly a loud, persistent clatter of rotors could be heard even above the mechanical din of the locomotive steaming down the line. Pete put down his shovel, leaning forward to study the blue canopy of cloudless sky through the cab's porthole window.

'That 'elicopter again,' he said, wiping his grubby face with the back of his hand. 'Second time today, Stan. Where's 'e goin' now?'

'Blowed if I know.'

The pannier tank drew into Bramley Cross station and visitors got out of the carriage, well pleased with their half-hour trip. As on other occasions, passengers will come along the platform and thank the footplate crew, and discuss the nostalgia of steam travel – how things were so much better

20

on the railways in the old days and how Dr Beeching had axed the branch, and road haulage had won the day. But it was ever so nice to see steam trains running again on the line. They were all united in this sentiment.

This morning Howard Sharp, a valued member of the preservation society and a grandfather who had brought along his little grandsons for a ride in the train, appeared alongside the cab and enjoyed a chat with Stan, the engine driver for the day.

'Brochure says Steam Open Day's the weekend after next. Good turnout expected. Money at the turnstile?'

'Well, Howard, providing the lovely weather holds out, I think we should just about break even. We've still got to finish restoring the station waiting room and there's tiles on the loco shed to fix before the winter lay-off.'

'Great news car-wise. Mike's finished buffing up his Morris Minor, and Ted's bringing his Ford Cortina, and there's an old MG Sports Tourer so beloved of the sixties being shown for the first time by Brian Jones.'

'The popular classic cars always pull in the punters. Any old buses this year?'

'Nope – not this year.'

'Fairground traction engine?'

'No – I wonder whether we shouldn't bend the rules a bit and feature Yank jeeps and Second World War army vehicles next year.'

'Now that's innovative. Sounds good to me. What about classic ice-cream vans?'

'Could do with one of those this morning. Blimey, it's hotter than the Sudan, even hotter than an Australian summer!'

A greasy, black-faced Pete, wiping his hands on a moist rag, shouted down from the footplate.

'Oy, Howard – coming to the meeting on Sunday? Special pow-wow ain't it? What's it all about? Brigadier Eames gathering his troops? The bloody continuing saga of the bridge that needs fixin', I shouldn't wonder. I mean, thirty grand for fixing a few bricks and heaving a couple of girders. I ask you – our ganger crew, most of 'em pensioners, could finish the job in a weekend. Bloomin' rail regulations, engineers' stipulations.'

'It's a stumbling block to our plans to relay the track bed as far as Fenley, construct new platforms and a station shelter, attract more visitors, build a picnic area. That's the way forward. Disabled loos is all very well, and paying for ramps for wheelchair access, but I'd rather spend what little money we have expanding the line.' Howard Sharp patted the children and got ready to head over the footbridge to the old two-berth caravan used as a temporary buffet on the up-line platform. 'Well, see you on Sunday. Cheerio.'

10

The distinctive BMW SUV was rumoured to be armour plated and its unusually thickly treaded tyres not only pothole-proof but bulletproof. The tinted windows allowed no possibility of making out the identity of the occupants but the fact that the Russian oligarch who had recently made Birchpark his home might actually be driving the powerful beast, or at least a passenger with bodyguards present, made each encounter more and more the subject of gossip amongst the residents of Bramley village. Was the SUV bomb-proof? Did the vehicle carry Kalashnikovs? In fact, the vehicle was owned by a well-to-do couple from London who were merely touring about both Bramley and Brocklehurst looking for a place for their grandmother to stay at weekends. In fact, the oligarch drove his new toy, an environmentally friendly electric super sports car, which Stan Clagg encountered that same morning cycling his bike up Station Road towards the Green Man public house on his way to the goods yard at Bramley Cross station. As he pedalled past he received what he perceived to be a friendly wave from whoever was positioned, low-seated, in the sports car, but it all happened so fast – in a flash.

'I wonder if it was him,' thought Stan, riding into the station forecourt. 'Was he parked here a minute ago? Hard to say.'

The powerful car was definitely a latest model. Stan

had read a review by Jeremy Clarkson in a colour supplement, damning its extortionate price and its non 'petrol-head' status. My God, how advanced had new technology become! Battery-powered mobility scooters and boyhood days of Scalextric – tiny wire brushes contacting the track to make the cars go round and round. Unbelievable! All in his lifetime. So you would surely need to be super rich to afford one of these high-performance cars powered by electricity. The Russian oligarch – it had to be him. Stan was sure as dammit that's who had passed him and waved.

'Yes, it must be him,' thought Stan, pushing his bike into the cycle rack before ambling along to the end of the platform, down the slope and heading for the loco shed, where he met Mr Regis, a normally dour and cadaverous individual who said virtually nothing and normally shunned conversation but was a volunteer in charge of locomotive overhauls and the restoration of carriages and wagon stock on the little railway. He was an accomplished engineer, albeit retired, and highly proficient at his job. He crossed the rusty tracks, his pipe clenched firmly between dentures.

'Hello, Stan, heard the news?'

'What, a text message?'

'Never mind texts!' Regis removed his briar-root pipe from his mouth. 'The bridge issue has been resolved. Work is to begin on repairing the structure. Trish from the buffet told me.'

'What marvellous news! At last – something more challenging than re-painting the waiting room and converting the toilets for disabled use. But who's coughing up the thirty grand, I'd like to know?'

'No idea.'

'A bridge no longer too far,' Stan chortled.

'Well, track-laying can start, it's only three miles or so to Fenley wildlife park and children's zoo. Once we hook up, build a picnic area and platforms, that's bound to attract more visitors to use the line.'

'Yep, bit of timber to start with, I reckon, will do for the platform. Hard to believe there was an actual station and signal box near there that British Rail in their great wisdom thought better to demolish. Well, we'll have to start from scratch, and that's that.'

'Fenley station – no longer a myth talked about by elders round their peat fires, a volunteer's far-off dream, seen only in old photographs. We're back and trains will be running again for the first time since BR deemed the line "no longer profitable".'

'And it's taken us fifty active volunteers, a private railway with a membership bordering three hundred over thirty years to put back what got lifted and carted off to the scrapyard. This really is the best news I've heard in a long while. I'll have to have a word with the brigadier. Are you coming to the meeting on Sunday?'

'I am, Stan. Now, I'd better get back to sorting out that luggage van. The woodworm's something terrible. The floor's the worst but the rest of it won't need too much repairing. Be seeing you, mate.'

11

The doorbell chimed. Mrs Clagg hurried along the hall, briefly paid attention to tidying her wavy hair in the gilt-framed mirror, and opened the door.

'Oh, Miss Parrish. What a surprise!'

'Why oh why must we be disturbed by that wretched low-flying helicopter, Vera? Is it something to do with that Russian oligarch? Is it really him, I wonder?'

'You know, I saw the news, pictures of the Olympic-sized swimming pool, the garage complex to house his fleet of cars, everything being altered and re-decorated. What a show!'

'Indeed, my dear, the *Gazette* carried a full-page spread on the new swish electronic, automatic gates to Birchpark Estate, as it's now called. The old gothic wrought iron monstrosities, I am glad to say, have been removed, along with those awful featureless pineapples that were fixed to the support pillars. He has taste at least.'

Miss Parrish, wearing strap-on sandals, a pair of cotton M&S slacks and a silky blouse ideal for summer wear, was ushered into the cosy sitting room and politely shown the sofa.

'How are your girls getting on? The International Young Musician of the Year competition is surely not far off. My, how time flies!'

'Yelena and Svetlana are being coached by Dame Moira Gorrie, the world renowned concert pianist. Her husband is putting Svetlana through her paces. He is a cello player,

26

so they are both getting the very best teachers, who are themselves experienced on the concert platform and understand the ways of top-rated orchestras. If only the country bus service was still running – Dame Moira's house is a bit out of the way and Dave's Cabs must be making a small fortune!'

'Yes, my dear, I do so miss the No. 36B into town. There was a rumour going round, wasn't there, that a rival bus company – Nevills' – would step in, but nothing's come of that so far. More of us appear to be using the Post Office store of late. Was that fresh farm produce I saw neatly displayed out front?'

'Yes, and thank goodness the prices have been slashed.'

'I believe Mrs Maggs was charging £3 for a dusty can of processed peas. She risked being shot or murdered at those prices. It was lucky she sold up when she did.'

'Well – and I say this in confidence – I believe Mrs Maggs did very well financially out of the sale of her business. The Post Office shop lives to fight another day. We have much to be thankful for. Is it the Russian, I wonder?' asked Mrs Clagg.

'Pardon me?'

'Responsible for all this investment in the village. I can't help thinking he was something to do with this.'

'You know Vera, one is reminded of the old ways of the gentry when the lord of the manor held sway. Such a nice, civilized man – Sir Jordan Croft, I mean. Of course, being a bachelor with no issue it all came to an end. Forced to sell the big house and vast tracts of the estate because it all became unmanageable. But one did so much like to see his black Phantom Rolls-Royce touring the lanes on his daily outings with the smartly turned-out chauffeur,' reminisced Miss Parrish.

'I hope you're not comparing this Russian billionaire with the landed gentry. I don't want to be lorded over by anyone, ta!'

'I am not comparing the old fiscal lord of the manor with anybody. Simply stating a fact that things were so much more "ordered" in those far-off days. One knew one's place. The old country ways were respected.'

'And there would have been a village constable to deal with those young people at the Green Man "Heavy Metal" nights.'

'Quite.'

'A glass of sherry, Miss Parrish?'

'Oh, that would be most kind.'

'I suppose Brigadier Eames is a sort of Lord of the Manor figure. He owns Notgrove Hall after all, and the village looks up to him.'

'He is certainly a most charming and courteous individual – a natural organizer.' Miss Parrish gratefully accepted her glass of sherry and paused for a moment. 'If a trifle—'

'If a trifle what?' asked a curious Mrs Clagg, sitting down again.

'Gentlemen of a certain age will be inclined to lavish unwanted attention on young ladies. Miss Clarke, the junior librarian, for instance. He will insist on presenting her with boxes of Belgian chocolates at every opportunity, when he takes his books back and so forth – yes, Miss Clarke...'

'Go on.'

'Oh, nothing remotely seedy or morally corrupt, but a man of over seventy shouldn't court a young lady like that. By showering her with gifts he makes himself seem foolish in the eyes of others, possibly open to ridicule.'

Mrs Clagg laughed. 'Perhaps your Miss Clarke is a gold

digger and encourages the old fool's advances. You know what? You'll read all of a sudden in the *Gazette* that they've got married and the next month he's being buried up at the church. And Miss Clarke's done very nicely for herself, thank you very much!'

'Somewhat fanciful, Vera.'

Sipping their Harveys Bristol Cream, the friends discussed more pressing issues, such as whether the Russian oligarch was married.

'No mention of a wife yet, but you never know. According to the local paper he has offices in Mayfair and an apartment in Belgravia, but fancied a country pile, so went ahead and purchased the Victorian asylum.'

'For a song, I should imagine. The Health Authority tried for years to sell it off, so he probably got the land cheap.'

'But an old asylum, home to generations of loonies!'

'Well, dear, it's isolated, secluded. One can only approach the extensive grounds through the front gates. And of course it was kept secure in the old days for fear the inmates, or rather patients, would escape and cause mischief. Thickly wooded, a lake, stoutly-built walls round the perimeter of the property – plenty of space for living accommodation.'

'For whom?'

'Bodyguards. An oligarch is surrounded with them these days. His support team – domestics, secretaries, drivers, pilots – they all have to be housed, my dear. Fed and watered. Take his enormous yacht moored in Venice along the bank of the Giardini. Apparently you cannot board the vessel unless you are wearing slippers supplied by, presumably, security personnel at the bottom of the gangway. No, there must be a small army of staff who are employed by the oligarch.'

'And the yacht has a bloomin' helicopter too, I believe.'

'Oh, he must own a fleet of helicopters. But he has the money, lest we forget, Vera. And I do wish that red one wouldn't make so much noise flying over the village.'

'I wonder what he's doing making circuits?'

'Why, Vera, isn't it perfectly obvious? Prying, taking aerial photographs, filming everything in sight. My property in Mouse Lane, your property.'

'Goodness, I'll have to have a word with Yelena and her sister. They sunbathe in their skimpy bikinis – sometimes topless – on the decking in our back garden!'

12

After visiting Mrs Clagg, Miss Parrish, whilst walking briskly towards the war memorial on her way back to her thatched cottage in Mouse Lane, encountered still more conversions taking place. 'Nancy's Tearooms', an establishment run for many years by the Sparrow twins Hilda and Mildred, was receiving something of a makeover, a gutting-out and refurbishment. The skip outside was overflowing with what remained of the Tudor frontage – smashed leaded windows, old bits of rolled carpet, the tassel-shaded brass wall lamps that used to hang inside, an upside-down cash register of the long extinct type.

The place was no longer evocative of a 1930s black and white Ealing Studios film set – a bygone era, quaintly archaic – but all modern, trendy, polished chrome, subtle shades of grey and green, and that was just the walls and bare fittings. Was that a kitchen area they were installing out back where the cramped porcelain toilets had been situated? Those chain-pull loos, those awful bowls ponging of bleach, and the shiny, hard toilet rolls that were so uncomfortable when used. Where were the Sparrow sisters now? she wondered. Where had they disappeared to? Their flat above the shop had its window frames knocked out and builders' tarpaulin in place of chintz curtains.

'Oh, I do beg your pardon,' said the inquisitive Miss Parrish, pausing before the steps and way-laying a strapping young carpenter, tanned and muscular, wearing a tool belt round his waist. 'Are the Miss Sparrows anywhere about?'

'Who?' came the blank response.

13

The new disabled toilets along the sunny platform were a cause for immense satisfaction. They had been brought in under budget and the important ramps and special bathroom fitments meant visitors to the railway using wheelchairs had better access at last.

The two-berth caravan on the opposite platform represented an eyesore. The plastic camping chairs and tables with shady umbrellas on poles were adequate, and in this lovely weather not too out of place, but that caravan serving buffet and teas had been propped up there along the platform for more than thirty years and it was definitely showing its age. The floor was wobbly and the seams leaking. The skylight had a lump of concrete on top to keep it from becoming detached and flying off in high winds.

Brigadier Eames chose to think positive. Stalin's special armoured train would be arriving on separate lorries and the locomotive was here already, standing in the yard awaiting transferral to the main siding, the red star emblazoned on its smokebox door evocative of Dr Zhivago, of high ranking Soviets and Siberian winters. The locomotive was damned impressive, more so than say the Flying Scotsman, and Thomas the Tank Engine – or even The Mallard.

At Sunday's meeting the brigadier announced the new Russian addition to the rolling stock, to be displayed on the siding, and everyone agreed it was certainly different and unusual. It was already causing interest from the press, and for the first time in living memory Jenny Frick, the glamour puss from *Southern Today*, would be doing a short feature which would appear on the local news programme.

At the meeting, members and volunteers were informed additionally of the news about the bridge. After maintenance work was completed and the bridge reinforced and passed structurally sound by inspecting engineers, track-laying could begin in earnest. This would not interrupt the summer train schedules because, at present, excursions terminated at Badgers Halt, where there was a chain-link fence across the line – a demarcation line, if you will – but not for much longer.

The bridge issue finally resolved was a cause for celebration and the ganger team, which included Mr Clagg, had just this week taken charge of an ex-BR steam crane to make the task of laying long sections of track considerably easier. A welcome gift of rusted rails already attached to sleepers was presently stacked beside the redundant signal box and this would be put to good use.

Steam Open Day loomed and, for the first time in many a long year, Brigadier Eames could see a light at the end of the tunnel, as it were. The little preserved railway appreciated locally was about to make its name. It was on the up at last!

After Sunday's successful meeting, Mr Clagg returned to his house for lunch cooked by his wife, Vera. While he tucked into his boiled cabbage and bacon, the girls Yelena and Svetlana chatted about the International Young Musician of the Year competition taking place in Cardiff and how Dame Moira was confident her talented charges would perform well on the bigger stage. They were both pretty – Russian beauties in fact. The exposure on television and the media coverage, even if you came last, was extremely valuable and the pair were very excited to be taking part in such a prestigious event. Their landlady, Mrs Clagg, proudly displayed a tin of beluga caviar on the table and some pickled herrings she had purchased specially at the Post Office store for sixty eight pence and forty pence respectively from the 'bargain of the week' basket.

The preparations for Steam Open Day were well under way. Apart from the trains, there was so much to do to ensure a happy and successful event. The weather was perfect, warm and sunny for the next week at least, so there was no problem there. The popular classic cars would be arriving on Saturday morning to line up in a row over at the field, the hot dog, burger, drinks and ice cream stalls were being set up. For the temporary shop selling railway magazines, books and souvenirs run by Mr Davies, the stripy awning, mallet, strings and pegs would need extricating from the canvas bag – an excruciatingly tight fit, a job that would take ages.

The girls Yelena and Svetlana would find time between their busy schedule of practice – Yelena the piano, Svetlana her cello – to attend the Steam Open Day at the little railway. They had not yet visited the Bramley Cross and Brocklehurst or travelled up to Badgers Halt on an excursion service so there was much to look forward to. Now they would not just be watching the chunky green and black engine with its single carriage and guards van steaming from afar, but actually be travelling on it.

14

On the Saturday Edie Blenchley visited her friend Miss Parrish at her thatched cottage in Mouse Lane for pre-lunch drinks.

A russet red brick chimney piece adorned with sparkling horse brasses dominated Miss Parrish's sitting room, and comfy but firmly-cushioned armchairs were positioned either side of a three-bar electric fire, one of Belling's earlier attempts at recreating a flickering coal flames effect. A once trendy G-Plan sideboard and shelves and a glass-topped coffee table helped set off the vast array of knick-knacks and collectables, including some Blue Spode and assorted chinaware, some of them quite valuable, which had been gathered over the years.

Over a glass of elderflower wine, ensconced in that little old lady's sun-drenched, commodious front sitting room, with its low, timbered ceiling, chintz curtains and sofa covers, various misgivings concerning the newly arrived billionaire Russian oligarch were discussed.

'It's his money, isn't it?' Edie offered.

'Whose money, my dear?'

'That oligarch – the Russian – it has to be his money. Who else could have bought out Mrs Maggs and the Sparrow twins so quickly and effectively?'

'Well, Edie, you know one person's money is surely as good as another's if it is invested wisely and judiciously. It is true we don't really know how this so-called oligarch obtained his billions – through legitimate means as a bona fide entrepreneur businessman? Or, perhaps, alternatively…'

'Alternatively how?' Miss Blenchley asked before sipping her wine.

'As a so-called gangster.'

'Oh, my goodness, Sybil, whatever do you mean? You can't mean – surely not – a crook?'

'Well, Edie, you only have to read the papers. Organized crime is on the increase everywhere these days, and the Russians are no exception. You see, there are various dodgy ways of obtaining vast sums of capital. In the old days the traditional lord of the manor held sway, but it's not as if they always used entirely honest or moral means to make their money – think about poorly maintained agricultural cottages or child labour. All illegal now, of course, but just accepted then.'

'You mean we should not care where this man's money comes from?'

'No, because it's none of our business.'

'And to think, Sybil, we now have a foreigner at the helm. That's what I mean, you see. Is it proper that a Russian should be – be taking over the village business infrastructure?'

'Now, now, Edie, I shall not brook with any form of racism. I have nothing whatsoever against the oligarch's country of origin. As I say, one person's money is as good as another's. No, this is nothing to do with that sort of racist, biased attitude. One merely wishes, out of interest, to know how he came to earn his billions, and that it is legitimate, above board, as it were. More elderflower wine, dear?'

'Thank you, Sybil. Oh, half a glass, I shall get tipsy otherwise. And now the cottage hospital.'

'A reprieve. Well, after all, we residents of Bramley signed that lengthy petition to the Health Authority. Brigadier Eames led a campaign, did he not? Public meetings, a march on the town hall at the end of last summer.'

'A reprieve? No, the Health Authority couldn't care less for our views on the matter. Closure was a certainty – until ... I hear it's been privatized, to be equipped with all the latest medical paraphernalia, a brand new maternity unit, outpatients. Is this his doing as well, I wonder?'

'It could well be. Now, Edie, I simply must go to the kitchen and fetch that roast saddle of lamb out of the oven. Would you be so kind as to prepare the mint sauce for me? Sprigs of mint fresh from the herb garden, olive oil and wine vinegar. So much preferable to that ready made jelly. Meanwhile, I shall lay the table.'

15

'Apparently a large garage complex is now complete in which to house his collection of the latest hot-metal, hand-built Ferraris, Lamborghinis and Rolls-Royce. He also owns a number of rare Porsche and a group of popular classic cars. A spokesman assures us that landscaping work is nearly complete and that the old asylum itself has been transformed into a family home. Birchpark Estate, as the house and grounds are now called, has been completed in record time and on schedule.'

Mr Clagg switched off the van's radio. In his Tupperware lunch box he had cellophane-wrapped sandwiches, a cut price pot of beluga caviar and a healthy yogurt purchased from the Post Office store. More and more people in the village shopped there these days. The range of seasonal local farm produce, fresh eggs and groceries could be bought as cheaply as at Lidl.

At the war memorial Stan swerved to avoid a brand new community bus filled with enthusiastic pensioners on their way to visit Lampley Castle, followed by lunch at a hostelry in the market town. The modern bus possessed a ramp that could be raised and lowered for passengers who were disabled and used wheelchairs. Another identical twin bus now operated a route into town where the old country line buses once ran.

It was Saturday afternoon and Mr Clagg was looking

forward to standing on the footplate of No. 2 engine, an 0-6-0 tank engine in British Rail livery called 'Delia'. As he turned into the yard he was gratified to find Steam Open Day progressing to plan. Hordes of visitors in summer shorts and floppy hats were pausing at the siding to admire Stalin's special armoured train, somehow vaguely menacing and resplendent at the same time, at present stationary, but it was easy enough to imagine it in motion, the engine emitting thick clouds of wood smoke as it steamed through the frozen snowy wastes towards Outer Mongolia, the grand black locomotive with a red star prominently displayed on the front being of particular fascination for children and adults alike.

Before taking up his duties at the loco shed to coal and fire 'Delia' for the late afternoon runs to Badgers Halt, Stan decided to soak up the atmosphere and take a stroll amongst the milling crowds of visitors. Folk queuing for the hot dogs and ices and fizzy drinks congregated over in the field where the popular classic cars were on display. He headed in that direction.

A raucous hoot echoed about Bramley Cross station as the little pannier tank engine started to pull out, hissing steam and smoke across the platform, the reek of burning coal and sulphur filling the warm, shimmering summer air, causing those who entered the station for the first time to be wonderstruck by the nostalgic, accurately restored décor. The printed tin advertisement boards for Wrights Coal Tar Soap and Liptons Tea and Players Cigarettes, the hand trolleys, the old luggage trunks, stationmaster and friendly porters dressed in period uniforms were of interest to old and young alike. Even babies in sun caps being pushed by mums seemed to like what they saw, waving their pudgy arms and wriggling their legs about excitedly.

Passing by the card table and chair allotted for collecting the entrance fee (50p), Mr Clagg heard a punter say quite loudly: 'That really takes the biscuit! An armoured train, here at the dear old Bramley Cross and Brocklehurst – who'd have thought it? A restored Esso wagon or a milk van on display, certainly – but an armoured train Stalin himself sanctioned. Oh my, that must be a first. The local press must be having a field day.'

'Talking of fields,' said his companion, taking off his sun shades, a wry look appearing on his bronzed features as he pointed his walking cane in the direction of the two rows of popular classic cars – 'what do you see? Mike's Morris Minor, Bill's Triumph Herald, Ted's Ford Cortina, Sid's Ford Popular, an Austin 7, a Humber Hawk, a Woleseley police car from the 50s, an old MG and . . .'

'Good grief, I don't believe this! Three immaculate, gleaming black limousines used by the likes of the Politburo in the bad old days of the Cold War. Kremlin taxis straight out of a le Carré Iron Curtain spy thriller. Russian ZiLs! Now where's my camera, I've just gotta get a picture of this, Rog.'

16

October and November had passed. Winter proper was here, summer – and the success of Steam Open Day – a long distant memory. Autumn was always a cherished time for Miss Parrish, who dutifully swept her lawn of dead leaves and heaped them onto her bonfire mound and, to the scent of gently burning leaves and crackling hedge cuttings, made sure her tubs and containers were tidy and garden tools cleaned and oiled properly and hung on their pegs in the tidy potting shed at the end of her cottage garden, and that the lawn mower was stored and its flex wound up. But it was now giving way to the cold dark nights of December, with progressively hard frosts. Last winter had seen rain, floods and gales, but this one was proving to be an icy affair due to freezing Arctic winds blown in from Siberia. Everyone in the village had remarked on the likelihood of snow and a long spell of cold weather. Department stores and shops in town were stocking plenty of fur hats and winter woollies, stout overcoats and ski anoraks, though a sturdy pair of fleece-lined winter boots was more Miss Parrish's priority. Thick rutted soles like tyre treads to prevent her, an old lady in her seventies, from slipping over and breaking her hip, a real danger for the elderly at this time of year.

She had met Stan Clagg in the Post Office store, who had in passing mentioned a policeman, of all people. A very forthright and intelligent young man, Inspector Robson was a volunteer on the preserved railway and started on a weekend course to become a fully-fledged engine driver. This involved plenty of work in the classroom of course, but it also meant he would be Stan's new partner on the footplate as a fireman, shovelling coal and helping out. To become a qualified engine driver, it must be stated, is part of a long apprenticeship, cleaning the ash pan, raking out the smokebox, etc. Well, the inspector had done all that, at least, so he, a policeman, was to be promoted to 'fireman'. Stan tried to make a joke of it, of course, but the humour passed over Miss Parrish's sensible head. But it certainly was unusual, a qualified detective from town being part of a train crew. Indeed, a precedent, surely.

Thoughts of furnaces and heat reminded the old lady she must check her Potterton boiler in the closet and adjust the thermostat for the cold nights.

During that evening, with lamps lit early, she was focused on knitting a scarf for her nephew's Christmas present, balls of wool by her side on the sofa, when her eye happened to rest on a pamphlet poking out from a pile of magazines – *My Weekly*, *Woman's Own* – resting on the second tier of her glass-topped coffee table. She paused from her knitting and held up the document to the lamp. It was the schedule for the Santa Specials running for the month of December, the week before Christmas in particular. Unfolding the neatly laid out brochure on her knee she studied it carefully.

17

Although Svetlana's cello playing had on this occasion failed to rouse the judges, it had been much appreciated by those in the auditorium and the TV audience alike. After all, she was a striking young woman, a delight to watch on stage performing. Yelena had fared better and came fourth with her outstanding interpretation of Mozart's Piano Concerto No. 2 in C Major K467. Dame Moira and her husband Leonard had been sitting in the front row and, when the judges' announcements came through, after praising the girl's obvious virtuosity, like the rest they stood up and joined in the raucous applause. At the end of the International Young Musician of the Year competition the girls were whisked away to a classy restaurant in Cardiff frequented, it was said, by Charlotte Church, where they basked in all the attention, particularly from a top agent who wanted the Russian pair on his roster of clients and promised them 'the world' if only they would sign, which, being sassy, they didn't.

Back in Bramley, things soon returned to normal. The pair were due to return to Moscow before Christmas and take up their studies at the Conservatoire when next term began. There was talk of Glyndebourne, but the girls were already committed to their tutors at the Moscow Conservatoire and they, as their father wished, would be staying put in Mother Russia for a while.

Mr and Mrs Clagg had watched the competition on

BBC2 and toasted their girls' success with a glass of iced vodka and a tube of Pringles.

Through October and November, when the preserved railway closed for the duration, Stan preoccupied himself with laying the new section of line to Fenley, including the bridge, as part of the maintenance crew who, with the assistance of the ex-BR steam crane, made good progress.

Winter services saw the running of trains limited to the Santa Specials outings in Christmas week – 'The Mince Pie Special', 'The Santa Claus Train', 'The North Pole Express' – the little green and black pannier tank with its red buffer beam would be busy, as would the black 0-6-0 BR liveried tank engine 'Delia'.

A new website had come into being, sprung out of nowhere – BramleyCross.com. Who had designed the site, let alone paid for it, was a mystery.

'We have to move with the times,' Brigadier Eames had mentioned casually when asked, modestly declining to comment on the superb layout, the excellent photos, and the stylish video footage.

As Yelena and Svetlana would not be returning to Russia until a couple of days before Christmas, although still practising, they had more free time and, on a girlish whim, the pair decided one morning at breakfast to volunteer as waitresses on the Santa Special when it ran a kitchen car and Pullman service for an evening trip, already sold out, on the 21st of December.

Mrs Clagg would be baking tray upon tray of mince pies on an industrial scale in the oven of her Aga range, well in advance of the Christmas excursion. The 21st Evening Special was the big one, the one everybody wanted to travel on.

18

Something of a stand-off had taken place. Having returned to Notgrove Hall, his gun-metal grey Corniche parked on the drive, he sat anxiously in his drawing room, curtains drawn, lamps on, nursing a large whisky and splash.

The brigadier had been driving his silver-grey Bentley, a car he had owned for years, which had proved consistently reliable and comfortable to travel about in. He had even on occasion driven it on the continent and hoped one day to take Miss Clarke, the junior librarian, for a spin. It gladdened his heart to think of a pretty young lady sitting in the front, settled comfortably on those broad, luxurious, calf-bound seats with the collapsible arm-rest, ash try incorporated, enjoying a trip round the lanes, finishing up perhaps at the White Hart just outside Brocklehurst, with their fine fish restaurant. At one time he recalled, like many of his generation, he actually liked to smoke cigarettes through courses. That would be frowned on now of course, smoking a cigarette while eating one's braised trout – really!

Back in the present, the stand-off. His Bentley Tourer had been rushing smoothly along that narrow lane, the one that hardly anyone knew about, which led off the dual carriageway and rose steeply up to the old asylum, now the Birchpark Estate. The car had come through the woods when he noticed with interest and, it must be said, some envy, the latest marque of Rolls-Royce, that wide, chunky modern bonnet, grille and fender, surface in the glare of his headlamps, the two vehicles taking up most of the road, each purring to a standstill, facing each other, grille to grille, the 'Roller' up against a Bentley Corniche of the old type.

Nonetheless, it was when four bright headlamps shone on his windshield, causing it to explode with light, and then dipped, allowing his vision to readjust, that he was astonished to see two powerfully built gentlemen leap out from the front seats of the ultra stylish Wraith. They wore immaculately cut and tailored Armani suits, and as they advanced towards his own car in long, galloping strides, he caught his first glimpse of what he was certain was a shoulder holster containing a weapon. There was no violence, the men were most courteous when they asked him who he was and where he lived. The taller of the pair requested him to kindly back onto the dual carriageway as it was a private road with night-time restrictions. Well he, the brigadier, an ex-army man, was not about to argue. He remained calm throughout the exchange, even gave them a friendly wave when he reversed back the way he had come. He was dealing with armed men, after all, men with guns who might be prepared to use them. They had been Russians all right, he was certain of that by their accents. The Cold War was over of course, the Iron Curtain melted, the Berlin Wall knocked down, but he had lived through all that, and what about organized crime? Russian gangsters? Could it be possible his friendly and benevolent oligarch, now the patron of his beloved Bramley Cross and Brocklehurst Preserved Steam Railway would be associated with those kind of people? Surely not...

19

'Oh, Edie dear,' said Miss Parrish, speaking into her landline phone which she propped on its stand. 'My Christmas pudding mixture is most satisfactory – the succulent raisins and sultanas and mixed peel I bought from the Post Office store. I always include half a squeezed lime and the zest of a lemon in my recipe, I find it enhances the flavour wonderfully. And a dash of brandy, of course. Who would have thought I could purchase a fresh lime at this time of year at the village shop? Only last winter, I recall, Mrs Maggs would have, say, a quantity of yellow-looking sprouts, a mouldy old cabbage well past its sell-by date, at most two or three baking potatoes, King Edwards that had started to sprout shoots, and a bag of over spongey tangerines in the display basket in front of the counter. How times have changed. Of course, I hear Mrs Maggs has bought a very nice new bungalow just outside Brocklehurst with the sale of her business... Do mind the sleet, my dear, and how cold it has grown of late... Yes, the nights close in so early in December. Such frosty mornings too. Goodbye.'

Miss Parrish glanced out of her window and saw Yelena and Svetlana, the Russian girls staying at the Claggs' house, race past on a pair of mountain bikes, scarves flying, pretty faces full of enjoyment.

At eleven o'clock the Revd Eaton, a young gadabout clergyman who took services both at the local parish church and at St Mary's in Brocklehurst, popped by to collect a bin liner full of washed sofa covers, rejected net curtaining and a ball of pink woolly night socks Miss Parrish had set aside for the jumble stall at the annual Christmas fayre held each year at the village hall. The vicar was enthusing about a sizeable donation he received from a benefactor who wished to remain anonymous, which would allow work to begin on fixing the leaking church roof. The lead needed replacing in parts and the present state of the roof meant every time it rained, buckets had to be placed strategically around by the brass eagle lectern and front pews. Work to fix the vaulted roof was long overdue, and praise be to God for this timely donation. The Revd Eaton also told the old lady he would be accompanying Mrs Quinn, a disabled parishioner who required a wheelchair, to the preserved railway on the 21st December, the evening of the Santa Special 'do'. He was very excited because they had Pullman seats and looked forward very much to riding on the train.

Miss Parrish, likewise, had booked up early and she and Edie would be seated together in the specially restored brown and cream dining carriage, pictures of which had appeared on the BramleyCross.com website, the vicar informed her. The enthusiastic young clergyman, over tea and biscuits, eulogized about old steam engines.

'Well, Vicar, I must say at the time they were regarded by many as dirty, smoky and not in the least cost effective.' But, yes, being of a certain age (she was now in her mid seventies), she fully understood the nostalgic draw of such aged industrial machinery. How sparkling these old locomotives now looked, after being saved from the scrap metal man's eager blow torch and meticulously restored to their former splendour by private lines such as the

'BC&B'. Livery polished and gleaming, GWR, British Rail, North Eastern, Caledonian and so forth. But back in the 1960s, when steam locomotion was being run down and replaced by diesel, Miss Parrish would not allow herself to wear rose-tinted spectacles as she recalled how filthy, unkempt and neglected steam engines appeared as they entered or ran through stations – goods, passenger service, main line express included. A despondent workforce, knowing change was inevitable and that diesel and electric motor units were here to stay, saw the era rapidly dissolving, being swallowed up by the vortex of historic time, the death of steam on the branch and main line workings...

However, just in the nick of time, along came the preservationists. Rotting and rusty engines got a new lease of life and now they could once more serve, but in all their glory, much care and attention lavished on them by enthusiasts like Mr Clagg. How wonderful that on these preserved railways a younger generation was presented with a polite and caring standard of service and clean and tidy stations few can actually recall from the 1950s and 60s. Branch lines transformed to a kind of railway idyll, in fact.

20

'It's that time of year again,' remarked Mr Minton, one of the volunteer fitters who was part of the restoration team responsible for rebuilding the Pullman carriage and kitchen car unit that would feature so prominently in the 21st December run.

He was perched on the buffer beam affixing a Santa Special nameplate to the top of the smokebox door of the 0-6-0 tank engine 'Delia', presently languishing in the shed behind the green and black pannier tank.

'The Santa Specials – I look forward to the North Pole run and meeting Father Christmas in his igloo at 8p.m.,' Stan joked, before stepping up onto the footplate. 'They've managed to paint and overhaul that Pullman car and the kitchen unit in time then.'

'Ooh, that must have been more than eight years we spent building them up from scratch – husks of rotten, mouldy wood when they first came to us. Lot of carpentry needed, refitting the panelling. Lovely job they did on re-covering the seats and reclaiming the original lamp fittings.'

'Looks a treat. Old Poirot would feel right at home sat at the table for luncheon service. Good as the Orient Express, I reckon!'

'That new BramleyCross.com has attracted a fair number of hits apparently. The video footage that you can activate at the press of a key is honestly breathtaking. Who on

51

earth came up with the money to design the site? Top-rate, nothing amateur about it, is there?'

'Our Santa Specials sold out weeks before – and we're getting enquiries about a souvenir shop which we haven't even the resources for yet. More members, more young volunteers, that's what we need. Someone even donated a whole lot of bloody fish plates and keys to help with the track laying. That never happened before the new website came on line.'

'My wife hates computers, but I says that's where everybody is now – on line. That's why nobody writes you letters any more. The Biro's practically redundant. But she won't listen.'

'Imagine if we hooked up with the main line again at Leasmarsh Spa. That's a long way off, of course, but we've got through to Fenley, despite that bridge. It's only ten more miles as the crow flies.'

'Yes, then trains from London can stop here – an all-the-way extension. Dream on, Stan.'

'So, despite British Rail ripping up the track and demolishing most of the stations and signal boxes all those years ago, a month or two to destroy the line, thirty years to put it back – we're in business. There's even talk of purchasing a Robinson designed Great Central 0-4 standard freight engine from another railway. Old Stalin's special armoured train certainly got us all excited! I'd love to have seen that big Russian loco running up the line. Next year perhaps.'

'Thank the Lord for Brigadier Eames. If those crucial decisions hadn't been taken early on, if it hadn't been for the foresight of those founding members, we never would have got where we are.'

21

The village had been suffering under a freezing pall of Siberian Arctic air for more than a week. Everything was frozen solid, fronds of frost literally solidified tree branches and hedgerows into whitened, rigid sculptures that twinkled at night under street lamps but by day remained motionless and brittle. The pavements remained skiddy and one had to be wary when venturing outside for fear of slipping over. The cold bit hard and froze your skin in seconds, making your face ache if not wearing a woolly balaclava or scarf protectively wrapped round you.

Indoors however was a different matter. The season of good cheer was, in Bramley at least, slipping into overdrive and in Mrs Clagg's case her Aga oven was baking mince pies from dawn 'til dusk, her prim and tidy kitchen the scene of mayhem. Pie tins, bags of flour, scales, measures of mixed fruit and peel – she was, with the help of Yelena and Svetlana, baking mince pies on an industrial scale with the express aim of feeding all the many passengers travelling to the North Pole on the Santa Special excursion train on the evening of the 21st.

Mrs Clagg's kitchen was agreeably warm, indeed the heat and seductive fruity smells of freshly baked pastries permeated the rest of the house. Her oven was working overtime, wire tray upon wire tray of cooling mince pies taking up every available space. Yelena was lining the pie moulds in the trays with pastry after wiping greasy butter-paper around, Svetlana adding dollops of sticky mincemeat with a wooden spoon. Then the pies were capped and glazed with a brush before being placed on the oven rack.

'Well done my girls,' said a pleased Mrs Clagg, wiping her pinafore with floury fingers, her plump features flushed, cheeks red from her proximity to the oven door. 'I'se reckon our quota is nearly done. Miss Parrish promised to bake a batch and I am assured Edie Blenchley will be popping round later with her oven readies. The mince pies must be at the station no later than half five. Mr Baxter, who will be in charge of catering once the train sets off, wants everything sorted in good time.'

'Erm, we have ourselves the itinerary in mind,' said Svetlana, glancing at her sister and slamming the oven door shut with a bang. 'We shall wear skimpy black waitress uniforms, yes, supplied by Mrs Blake, and also pointy Santa hats with flashing lights.'

'You'll both look adorable,' chuckled their landlady. 'Mind you, don't get your bottoms pinched too often. Working along the aisle when a train is in motion, in close proximity to red-blooded male passengers full of good cheer, requires managing your bottoms carefully. I can assure you from past experience you'll both be rushed off your feet, so it means you must be extra careful not to spill mulled wine in the laps of table sitters. It will require a level of tact and politeness, and strong nerves to walk up and down making sure everyone has enough mince pies and that their glasses are topped up.'

'My goodness,' said Yelena, 'half past four already. We'd better get ready.'

'I'll make us all a nice cup of tea,' said Mrs Clagg, watching her charges tear upstairs to change.

22

On the afternoon of the Santa Special event, the light starting to fade and lamps lit early, Brigadier Eames sat on the sofa sipping sherry at the thatched cottage in Mouse Lane belonging to the spry little old lady, Miss Sybil Parrish. He stretched his legs in front of the electric synthetic coal fire, adorned on either side of the hearth by a polished brass coal scuttle, fire tongs and a knobbly poker and coal brush. Then, putting down his glass on top of the coffee table, the old soldier took out his pipe and matches.

'Men with guns,' he frowned intently at the fake flickering flames.

'Guns? Really, Brigadier, that's absurd. My nephew tells me that iPods, Googly Tablets and wotnots now have leather carrying cases. They're very much like holsters, aren't they? Were you not perhaps mistaken? After all, you have already explained that four startling headlamps flooded your car with blinding light for a moment or two before being dipped. You were dazzled, unable to see clearly.'

'Oh, I was only partially dazzled.' The brigadier placed his trusty briar pipe in his mouth and struck a match. 'No, no, no – what I saw was clearly a gun holster. The fellow's jacket flapped open when he got out of the Rolls-Royce, and there it was! I saw it.'

'Not one of these cash 'n cough wotsitsnames?'

'Not a Kalashnikov, no, that's an automatic self-firing

55

rifle. This was some sort of a hand gun – I'm certain of it.' He blew out a cloud of wafting smoke and settled back on the sofa again.

'But if these men were his assistants, surely mobile phones would be requisite, else walkie-talkies?'

'Bodyguards,' the brigadier corrected, smoking his pipe thoughtfully. 'And when I saw that fella stepping out of the Rolls 'Wraith', neglecting to button his suit jacket properly, highlighted by the clear glow from both sets of dipped headlamps, it was some sort of pistol I saw. No, no, no, not a mobile phone or a walkie-talkie. Of course, they were very polite, there was no question of me being bullied in any way.'

'But they achieved what they wanted.'

'Precisely.'

'Which was to make sure you reversed back down the lane onto the dual carriageway. Cleared off, to put it crudely.'

'Men with guns!' The old soldier muttered, putting down his pipe and taking a sip of sherry.

'Men with iPods, Googly Tablets or mobile phones,' Miss Parrish insisted with a firm intonation to her voice. 'You referred earlier to organized crime and the Russian Mafia. Can anyone tell me how the oligarch actually made his billions? I mean, was it earned legitimately?'

'I'm beginning to seriously wonder,' declared the old gentleman, frowning, at least grateful for this chance to chat openly with Miss Parrish at her cosy little cottage and 'clear the air' a bit. 'But I must emphasize I have much to be grateful to him for,' he confessed. 'And I shall in no way be rocking the boat or ruffling his feathers, Miss Parrish.'

'Oh, why's that?'

'He is the new benefactor for our railway, and is now represented on the board of directors. With the new cash injection we shall be able to afford a new station buffet, a souvenir shop, the reintroduction of the old Bramley Cross signal box, levers and frames fitted, new signalling along the track and a brand new station at Fenley. No, I am not complaining, Mafia links or no.'

23

At a quarter to six, excited visitors to the little preserved railway crowded the 1950s period painted and furnished ticket hall, chatting and milling about; the Santa Special was running late but fully booked.

The hatted and overcoated vicar, the Revd Eaton, the young and gangly clergyman with the ostrich neck and wobbly Adam's apple, was pushing Mrs Quinn in her wheelchair. She wore a gay red scarf and red floppy hat adorned with a sprig of plastic holly. They managed to progress through the entrance onto the platform proper, the length of which was lit by a row of hissing Tilley oil lamps hung from the station awning.

The excursion service for the evening's Christmas event was in: the 0-6-0 tank engine 'Delia' up at the front of the train, which consisted of one passenger carriage, a Pullman coach and a kitchen unit and guards van. The locomotive had its metal sign 'THE SANTA SPECIAL' prominently displayed over the smokebox door, her red buffer beam clean and gleaming. A loud toot-toot of train whistle and the trill of a porter's whistle announced imminent departure. Doors were slammed, everybody hurried on board to take their seats. In the case of the posh Pullman coach with its table seats, each table was decorated with a paper plate full of assorted chocolate bars and festive crackers. Everyone travelling on 'The Special' that evening was presented with a surprise gift pack containing themed Christmas card, vouchers, a little route map and a brochure for next year's events commencing in Easter week.

Miss Parrish and her friend Edie Blenchley sat in aisle seats opposite one another with a good view of proceedings. Miss Parrish duly noted everyone coming on board, the young and the old alike. Waitresses squeezed through, assuring people and generally fussing and making sure everyone was comfortable. She recognized the pretty, leggy Russian girls, Yelena and Svetlana, bustling down the aisle and thought their flashing Santa hats most fun and festive. Brigadier Eames sat at the end table with a number of staff and volunteers, evidently enjoying himself, pulling a cracker. An obese gentleman wearing an immaculate double-breasted grey suit waddled along and slumped politely in his window seat, chatting amiably with a mother and her two children.

At this point there was a clumping of couplings, and the Pullman coach seemed to lurch forward. The waitresses kept steady feet and continued handing out festive mince pies from a serving tray, which were gleefully consumed, particularly by the under eights, of which there was a fair profusion. Couplings again bumped, and after a particularly raucous blast of train whistle that boomed about the station and its immediate vicinity, even as far as the war memorial, the Father Christmas train, the Santa Special, departed on time for the North Pole – or, to be more precise, Badgers Halt.

Up front there would be no rest for Mr Clagg or his fireman for the run, the detective chappie, or rather trainee engine driver, Mr Robson. With his trusty shovel he heaved lumps of coal into the firebox, back-breaking work and bound to keep him fit. Stan adjusted the regulator and kept his eye on the track stretching up past the redundant brick signal box. Pressure was building up and the train rattled along, the footplate of the 0-6-0 tank engine 'Delia' squealing and rumbling like the other riveted parts of the loco as it slowly gathered speed and shot through a cutting.

It had been snowing earlier and, what with the cold Siberian weather of late that froze everything in sight solid, the surrounding fields and hedgerows were patchy white and glittered as the train, with its row of lighted carriages, passed along the post and wire fence. The steady chuff-chuff-chuff of the tiny tank engine up front filled the night air as the Santa Special made good progress towards the North Pole. Everyone on board the train was laughing and chatting, filling their faces with chocolate and warm mince pies washed down with beakers full of mulled wine or fizzy orange dispensed by the waitresses dashing to and fro along the aisle from the kitchen unit.

'Is your nephew visiting for Christmas?' asked Miss Blenchley as a waitress hurried past bearing a jug of mulled wine precariously above her head.

'Well, my dear,' said the old lady in confidence, 'I must tell you, frankly Wilberforce will dilly-dally and procrastinate right up to the last minute. In early October he assured me he would be arriving on Christmas morning before church. At the end of November I am told he will arrive on Christmas Eve with his new girlfriend Jessica and stay until Boxing Day only. His latest epistle informed me he will in fact not be bringing his girlfriend and he will be staying a full week! Well, Edie, I shall have to prepare breakfast, lunch and tea for a full week which puts me out as it's a lot of extra food to put on the table.'

'And there's cocoa to buy, of course. Young men do so like their bedtime drinks.'

'Oh indeed, dear me—' Miss Parrish blanched noticeably. 'Don't look now but someone's fainted. No, don't turn round, no need to be unnecessarily inquisitive.'

Miss Parrish, seated where she was with a special view of the carriage, had observed a concerned waitress, Yelena, calling anxiously for the head steward. The person who had collapsed was the overweight fellow in the grey suit. She tried to distinguish the various persons huddled round the table. Brigadier Eames was being kept informed by another waitress. Miss Parrish was glad to see Yelena had now got a grip on herself and was back smiling and passing along the row with a jug of mulled wine in one hand and orangeade in the other, her Santa hat flashing merrily.

'Is there a doctor or a nurse in this carriage?' queried the head steward, getting out his mobile phone and a walkie-talkie hitched to the belt of his trousers. Most passengers paid little heed and continued munching their mince pies, regardless of a little 'incident' going on. The Pullman was crowded, after all.

Miss Parrish, craning her neck, caught a fleeting glimpse of the bulk of the obese man collapsed over the table. Unfortunately he looked unhealthily grey and dead, but she couldn't be sure. It was hard to tell at this distance, peering over people's heads to get a better view. Mrs Adams, a staff nurse in the maternity unit at the cottage hospital who luckily was on board, hastened down the narrow aisle, bumping into Yelena coming the other way, and was able to make a cursory examination. The poor, ill man briefly rose up but was violently sick – so he was not dead at least.

Miss Parrish and Edie Blenchley distinctly heard Mrs Adams say, 'Something he ate – a stomach upset – but we need to be sure it is nothing more serious. Get the cottage hospital to send the paramedic car and ambulance. Since it became privatized we have much more resources, including an examination room, so he won't peg out on us, I'm pretty sure of that. If we can just move him along to the kitchen car unit's toilet and keep him out of sight.'

'Of course,' said the chief steward irritably. 'Peg out? He can't do that – not during Christmas week on the Santa Special.'

24

The locomotive was stationary – job done. Inspector Robson had been purloined by a spry little old lady waving her brolly at him to gain his attention on the footplate. Despite her years she had made every effort to clamber onto the cab step to be fairly level with him. The Santa Special had been in the platform for some ten minutes, passengers disembarking, coming up to say hello, commenting on the nostalgia of good old steam travel and now her! There had apparently been someone taken ill with a tummy bug on the train but the trip to the North Pole to see Santa in his igloo had passed smoothly, and everyone had an enjoyable time. Except, it would seem, for this pushy, persistent woman.

The blue strobe lamps of the ambulance in the station forecourt only enhanced the festive mood. The paramedic car, a slim BMW, also had its lights flashing, the effect being to make the frozen, snowy station precincts even more evocative of Antarctica. No one crowding out of the ticket hall was any the wiser about the person who had apparently collapsed after eating a mince pie.

Robson, although a detective from town, was off duty and in no hurry to become involved. This was not a police matter, he insisted. Let the medics get on with it, they were professionals, after all, and it appeared Mrs Adams had everything under control.

'Would you be good enough to pop round to my

63

cottage in Mouse Lane, Inspector?' said the energetic old lady, not taking 'no' for an answer. 'I mean to say, I must talk to you in your official capacity. My name is Sybil Parrish, I live quite near the station round by the war memorial. It will only take you ten minutes to walk, after all. Mouse Lane, is that clear?'

'Very,' replied the off-duty officer, leaning against his coal shovel, humouring the old dame. 'Just give me a chance to change out of my work overalls and spruce up in the wash-room – I'll be about an hour. I'll be there, I promise, but I must tell you,' he shrugged, glancing at Stan who was also on the footplate listening in, 'people are taken ill, even on a holiday excursion. They eat something that disagrees with them, are perhaps allergic.'

'I can say no more at this juncture, Inspector.' The elderly woman, perhaps in her mid-seventies, hurried off along the now almost deserted frozen platform with her friend, Edie Blenchley. A sheeted stretcher supporting the weight of the ill, obese man had passed through the ticket hall some twenty minutes earlier, the ambulance and paramedic car were nowhere to be seen.

25

'Why oh why do I think of the Litvinenko case, Inspector – a Russian gentleman poisoned in the heart of London?'

'Yes, he ingested a fatal dose of polonium. The circumstances surrounding the case are still unclear. We all saw it unfolding on the television news, didn't we? A possible act of nuclear terrorism on the streets of London. We're not honestly comparing a serious crime like that to a man with an upset tummy, taken ill on the train, are we?'

Miss Parrish was interrupted and unable to reply when her mobile began lighting up and vibrating on top of the coffee table. She snatched the phone and held it to her ear, listening intently.

'Edie dear, the ill gentleman was taken to the cottage hospital, you're sure of that? You're parked outside? Did you talk to anybody? That nice Ghanaian doctor, Mr Tomkins, what did he have to say? Not much? Oh well, and Edie be good enough to meet me outside my cottage in twenty minutes. Oh yes, there'll be plenty of time for a cup of tea later.'

'Admitted to hospital – does that sound like a stomach upset to you? A tummy bug? Really, Inspector, this is far more serious. I saw that man, he looked grey and dead – not just taken ill – the waitress looked very shocked indeed.'

'Pardon me, Miss Parrish, his symptoms need not be suspicious. He was obese after all, overweight.'

'What's being fat got to do with it?' Miss Parrish answered, somewhat tersely. 'He was a Russian, Inspector.'

'How do you know this?'

'Because he was in conversation with one of the waitresses, Yelena. They were chatting and joking together, speaking in fluent Russian, Yelena herself being from that part of the world.'

'So he's a Russian. What does that prove?'

'He seemed to me a gentle giant, a friendly great bear of a man, a large bulk certainly, but most polite and considerate to others. He boarded the Pullman coach with a steady step, allowing several ladies to pass before finally taking his table seat. Are you or are you not, Mr Robson, going to become involved in this affair – in your official capacity as a detective of police, I mean?'

'I have no reason to, Miss Parrish,' he said in a determined, no nonsense way. 'As I told you, a gentleman takes ill on board a train – that does not constitute a serious crime.'

No doubt about it, the detective from town had had more than enough of this tough, little, elderly spinster and her determined ways. He got up to leave.

'Well, if you'll just excuse me, Inspector, I have rather urgent correspondence to attend to. Oh dear me, yes, I'm afraid I do not share your easy views. I am of the strongest impression the gentleman may have been deliberately poisoned. Now, where are my Clintons notelets?'

26

At nine o'clock a Ford Fiesta pulled up outside the cottage in Mouse Lane. A few flecks of snow blew about under the glare from the street lamp. The pavements, just as they had been through the day when it was almost as cold, were icy and perilous under foot. Miss Parrish, on realizing her friend's car had drawn up outside, adjusted her woolly bobble hat in the hall mirror, wrapped her scarf tightly around her and prepared to face the chilly outdoors. Closing the door behind her, she stepped cautiously along the paved path with its myriad frozen footprints, and made it to the front gate in one piece. She held an envelope containing her note greedily to her chest and, with a little assistance from Edie Blenchley, was soon seated in the front of the car, a warm air heater blowing comfortably about her legs.

'Where to?' asked Edie, peering in the rear view mirror and driving off.

'Birchpark Estate, the home of the oligarch, that's our first port of call.'

'You're surely not intending to see him! These people require appointments, don't they? I mean, you're not one of his personal acquaintances, a family member.'

'Oh my dear, I only meant to post a letter. These places have an outside letter box, don't they? I mean, how on earth does Mr Radley, our postman, deliver letters up there – by bicycle?'

'A post van, Sybil. What about the security cameras, will they have fitted them yet at the entrance gates?'

'The first thing they did, I shouldn't wonder. Oh, they're everywhere these days, the town's full of them, peering down as you walk along the high street. A few more won't matter. Anyhow, we've nothing to hide. I'm merely delivering a letter – an urgent one.'

Driving from the turn-off up the rise to the gates, the ladies encountered no rush of bodyguards, sinister Rolls-Royce cars or trigger-happy members of the Russian Mafia. The Ford Fiesta drew up outside the electronic gates. Lights automatically switched on, bathing the area, but there was nothing untoward about this. Many households possess such devices.

All seemed quiet. An owl hooted from the direction of the frozen, snowy woods. One set of footprints led to the post box incorporated in the pillar at the side of the electronic gates – and back again to the parked car. Those of a determined Miss Parrish. It was only when the Ford Fiesta sped off into the darkness that a person trudged down from the house, unlocked the back door of the post box and removed its contents, peering up into the lens of a concealed security camera as he did so.

27

The second port of call for the ladies was the home of Mr Edwards, a retired physics master who had been a teacher and head of the local comprehensive over at Adderton for many years until retirement several years ago. He lived in a nice, modern bungalow in Larch Close, one of a neat, prim little square of detached houses. The lights were on. Another inch of snow had fallen since seven o'clock that night. The garage and the roof and front garden of the bungalow were covered in a thick crust of soft white snow. Vaporous smoke rose from a chimney next to a TV aerial.

Miss Parrish promptly trudged up the path and rang the doorbell. Chimes sang out from within. A shadow loomed behind frosted glass and suddenly there was the tall, imposing figure of Mr Edwards, wearing a bow-tie, cardigan and neatly pressed trousers. His crinkly bronzed face broke into a wide grin.

'Why, Miss Parrish, how delightful to see you. I see Edie's waiting in the car. Have you come about the jumble leaflets?'

'Oh, the jumble sale – no – I wonder, Mr Edwards, if you have in your possession a device for measuring radioactivity, such as a Geiger counter? Is that what they're called, or is that all old hat now? If so, I wonder if I might borrow it?'

'A Geiger counter, good Lord. If you'd allow me to put

on my gum boots I'll come and open up the garage where I keep my boxes of odds and ends. I did have one, a Geiger counter, that is. The instrument was used for demonstrating the measurement of the intensity of ionizing radiation in the school lab. Sixth formers found the instrument absorbing. During lessons we would discuss scenarios of harmful levels of radiation and its effects, and so forth.'

'How does it work exactly?'

'Basically you hear it emit a crackling noise that intensifies in frequency. A measuring gauge tells you what the level is. The needle darts to red for dangerous levels, of course.'

'Is it easy to use, or do I have to be a scientist?' she asked, recalling the popular *Quatermass* television series.

'Ah, a child could operate one, my dear. There's a light-weight power pack with a shoulder strap, and an on-off switch. Press it on and away you go. Couldn't be simpler.'

The freezing garage area was lit by a single bulb. Amongst the usual clutter of coiled leads, power mower, anti-freeze and tools, Miss Parrish spied a mountain bike, de-chained and with its gears hanging off, leaning against a stack of cardboard boxes. This was removed by Mr Edwards and wheeled to one side so that he could get to his box, inside of which was a record deck, a Phillips 8-track cassette player and old wooden speakers trailing wires. He rummaged about for a bit.

'Of course, mobile phones, CD players and microwave ovens emit small amounts of radiation. Is that what you want to measure? If so...'

'Just to check the levels in my kitchen, Mr Edwards, to put my mind at rest. One reads so much about the unseen effects of using mobile phones. Those ugly masts, the health risk.'

'But the risk is minimal, Miss Parrish. We're not going to start glowing in the dark, you know.'

The retired physics master ripped off a strip of duct tape from a thin box he had recovered, pulled out a power pack and the Geiger counter and handed it over to the old lady, deciding it best not to argue with her and let her borrow the instrument. A child could use it without breaking it, so why not her?

'Oh, thank you so much, Mr Edwards,' she said, taking out her purse. 'May I offer you a five pound note for its hire?'

'I wouldn't dream of taking your money, Miss Parrish. Just take care of the instrument, my dear; I believe it's energized so you won't need to re-charge the power assembly for some time.'

28

The cottage hospital, the ladies' next destination, lay on the outskirts of the village and, during the last month, had become unrecognizable.

Built during the Second World War, the hospital was mostly pre-fabricated. Mossy, lichen-stained, corrugated iron roofs, blotchy pebble-dash-coated walls or plaster board, ill-fitting window and door frames, a Nissan hut joined on, used for the maternity unit, everywhere leaking and draughty, acres of faded wartime linoleum. Yet despite its construction faults, this NHS outpost had for years successfully served the villages of Bramley and Brocklehurst. It was really a collective of shanty-shacks that had for decades been well attended, a vital centre for medical health care in the community. So when it was announced that closure was imminent there was a public outcry: meetings, marches, demonstrations and a petition, all of which proved pointless, for the Health Authority had still wanted to close the unit.

Then came private medical care. Out of nowhere, it seemed, a new block was built, the old pre-fabs confined to the bonfire. A parking area, smart outpatients' department, surgeries, operating theatre, child care facilities, reception – and this modern facility was where Edie Blenchley and Miss Parrish were sitting outside in the car watching the various comings and goings with growing interest.

For starters, a large articulated lorry had arrived and

parked in the forecourt. There was a great deal of activity inside the place. People could be seen dashing to and fro behind the clear plate-glass frontage. An oblong metallic container had been ushered into reception, swiftly and efficiently, and now it was being placed in the back of the articulated lorry.

'I suspected as much,' said Sybil Parrish sombrely, handling the power pack out of a Tesco's carrier bag, the warm air blowing about from the car heater. She passed her best friend a boiled mint, all the while referring to the crackling noise being emitted by the Geiger counter balanced on the dash. The ladies continued to access the peculiar events unfolding over at the cottage hospital. 'Inspector Robson just has no idea. Do you know if there is an intensive care? Do these places offer such facilities?'

'I've no idea, Sybil. They've certainly upgraded the care here, these private health people.' She sighed and wiped the misty condensation off the windscreen with a cloth before replacing it in the dashboard compartment, snapping it shut. 'But look what they're wearing!'

'Those suits are for a purpose. Now, Edie, I don't want you to be alarmed or to panic in any way, but frankly those people are wearing all-in-one CBRN – *chemical, biological, radioactive and nuclear* – protective suits against contamination. The presence of this enormous lorry and that metal container offers a portent.'

'An alert.'

'Quite. If my instincts are proved correct, there is a man in that metal box, quite probably dead, the same gentleman taken ill on the Father Christmas train earlier this evening. Just listen to that thing crackling on the dash, the needle is certainly in the red. There is, my dear, a palpable trail of radioactivity being emitted from reception.

Oh, I'm sure we are well clear of it ourselves, but it is present in the area of the cottage hospital, nonetheless.'

'What if he'd suffered a heart attack?'

'Why the space suits, all this busy-bodying about? No, we are witness to a contamination threat of some kind. I am inclined to favour polonium, but we shall see.'

Even when the Ford Fiesta sped off, the crackling noise from the Geiger counter did not cease until they were at the end of the lane and turning off to head for the village.

29

Not surprisingly, Miss Parrish could not sleep. At half past two she got out of bed and reached for her mobile phone. She punched for directory enquiries and a pleasant Indian voice, a lady, answered. As requested, she put Miss Parrish through to the Atomic Weapons Research Establishment at Aldermaston. The call went through and there was the usual ringing tone.

'Yes, can I help?' asked a male voice on the other end – kindly, patient, yet also cautious.

'Might I be put through to someone who could help clear up a few points regarding radiation contamination for me? I'm new to this science and a little confused about the effect of polonium.'

'Are you by any chance engaged on an Open University course – a mature student?'

'How perceptive of you, young man. You know, I've been up practically all night thinking through a problem.'

'Hang on, I'll put you through to Dave Bates, I'm sure he'll be able to sort you out.'

'Hello, night duty, Professor Bates speaking.'

'Polonium – could I detect it on a Geiger counter?'

'You would find no gamma radiation. Polonium emits alpha particles that can only be detected by sophisticated tests. If ingested it goes straight into the gut and stomach. It is highly difficult to detect.'

'That's most kind. I'm very grateful for your succinct

explanation, Professor Bates, and I'm so sorry to bother you at such a late hour. Do thank that nice young man who answered the phone earlier. My OU science thesis shall be much enriched for our conversation.'

'No bother.' The line went dead.

Miss Parrish leaned over and parted the curtains, peering out of the window at the snow falling outside, gently pattering against the pane, gathering on either side of the lintel. She drew her nightgown comfortably about her, pulled on an old Fair Isle jumper, and hurried downstairs to boil a pan of milk for a malt drink. The Potterton boiler was rumbling away in the closet and her central heating turned up. All was warm and cosy in her little cottage, just as it should be. But what of that Russian gentleman, what had become of him...? Or his radioactive body, at least. The matter of the unlikelihood of polonium being present, the man's death being attributed to some other deadly nuclear contaminant, bothered her. So polonium was out ... but what exactly was in?

30

Miss Clarke, the junior librarian, an attractive blonde with a fine pair of legs and winning smile, while looking up Amazon on her computer to check out a new biography for a customer, noticed a very tall, broad-shouldered man in a gabardine mac pausing at shelves over by the crime section. He wore a trilby and was deeply tanned. He gasped with pleasure as he evidently spied an author he liked. Gathering four or five hardback books to his chest, he swiftly advanced towards the counter. Miss Clarke was free and, placing the pile of books in front of her, the tall gentleman pulled out his wallet.

'I'm so sorry,' he said in broken English, 'I am new round here. Do I need a pass – to pay?'

'Oh, a library ticket. That's really no problem. Have you some identification? A bank card will do. There's no charge.' She took down a few details on her computer, asked him to sign the slip of plastic and it was all done.

The old fellow seemed delighted with his new library card. Once the books were scanned he took off his trilby and bid her good day, heading for the automatic door, his pile of crime novels clustered in a carrier bag. The thick, heavy gold watch he wore on his deeply bronzed wrist was a Rolex with a blue face. His bank card had been a platinum American Express, the most prestigious of the lot.

Miss Clarke sighed. The automatic door swung open

and in waddled Brigadier Eames, bearing gifts. What a wretched nuisance! Action stations! She swiftly handed over to Dorothy, a senior member of staff who worked mornings at the little village library, and went out back to help Mrs Evans, her supervisor, catalogue some new stock, and sort out the weekly book delivery by the county van. Before she hastened away she recalled the name and address of their latest library member: Oleg Petrovich, Birchpark Estate, Bramley.

31

There was no mention on the *Today* programme, or on television news that morning, of a Russian dying, a contamination alert, or of any conspiracy to murder a passenger on the Santa Special.

Miss Parrish decided to call on Mrs Clagg before returning the Geiger counter to Mr Edwards at his bungalow in Larch Close. Mr Clagg, Stan, would of course be occupied on the preserved railway, operating the last of the Santa Special excursions due that year before the line closed for winter. It would not open again to the public until Easter.

'My dear Miss Parrish, how lovely to see you. Yelena and Svetlana caught the coach down to Heathrow early this morning from town. We saw them off at the coach station. The flight to Moscow leaves Heathrow this afternoon. They'll soon be 20,000 feet up in the air watching in-flight movies and enjoying those gantry cooked microwave meals that the stewardesses wheel along the aisles in tin trolleys.'

'And what delightful, intelligent girls! We shall all miss them, my dear, and to think, dear little Yelena coming fourth in the competition. Her parents shall be so proud of her.'

'Their papa rang yesterday to thank me – wants Stan and me to visit Moscow, have a holiday there and stay with them at their apartment. Such a friendly man.'

'Excuse my prying, Vera, I don't mean to be nosey, but what does "papa" do for a job exactly?'

'Why, he's a very high-up chap in petroleum refining, I think Svetlana said. A real clever clogs, if you will.'

'Clever clogs indeed, my dear. Now, I've got two dozen mince pies I baked for the afternoon Christmas Special, snug in their Tupperware box. Where shall I put them?'

'Oh, come through to the kitchen, Miss Parrish. You can plonk them on the table. My, it's so quiet without the girls. There's talk of Glyndebourne next year if their studies at the Moscow Conservatoire permit. Here, I'll put the kettle on and make us a nice pot of tea. Stan tells me the new BramleyCross.com website is proving popular and receiving a number of hits every day.'

'Hits?' queried the old lady, totally bemused, finding the absorption of computers totally wasteful.

'Ah, people browsing the web are able to contact the preserved railway and find out about its history – the train times, events and so on. A hit refers to, well, you know, how you punch a number on your mobile phone.'

'Oh, yes, I see. Vera, my dear, what a relief to put down all of these carrier bags.'

The ladies entered the prim and tidy kitchen. Outside the window, wild birds clustered around the wire feeder, squabbling and pecking furiously at the nuts. It was evident Mr Clagg had at some stage that morning made an effort to scrape the path, but this had proved futile due to the continued cold weather and fresh falls of snow.

A loud, persistent crackling noise started up. At first, Miss Parrish naturally focused on the Roberts portable radio on the sill, thinking it to be some sort of static being emitted by a speaker. Mrs Clagg looked around the room in amazement, trying to trace where the crackle was coming from. But a growing awareness overtook Sybil Parrish when she realized the crackling noise was coming from one of her Tesco carrier bags – the one containing the power pack and Geiger counter she would be returning later that morning to Mr Edwards. The noise only intensified over by the Aga, the oven in particular, and as Miss Parrish walked slowly round the kitchen, still clutching her carrier bags, a clack-clack-clack-clack-clack-clack issued loudly as she neared the shelf with the metal baking trays. She hastily found the OFF switch on the power pack, which she had accidentally triggered when she was swapping bags around, but she had noted a strong gamma count existed in Mrs Clagg's kitchen.

'Oh, silly me,' she laughed. 'You know, Vera, it's one of those ceiling heat detector whatsits. I'm taking it to the electrical shop in town, it keeps going off for no reason.'

Mrs Clagg seemed more than satisfied with the explanation and hurried over to switch on the electric kettle, busying herself with tea bags and a couple of mugs.

32

The village library, despite the cold weather, was fairly busy, and Brigadier Eames had skulked over by the travel section, hoping to catch a glimpse of Miss Clarke and take his books over to be scanned in one swoop, offering her the beautifully wrapped carton of Belgian chocolates he had bought specially, the neatly tied ribbon, gold packaging bound to impress the girl. But no sign of Miss Clarke did he see – only that old biddy, the one who lived locally and worked mornings. Dorothy wasn't she called – Dorothy or Patricia, something like that. He was becoming more and more impatient. He held on for another five minutes and, when he could bear the suspense no longer, replaced the books and left, promising to himself that he would return later that afternoon.

It was always a treat to spend time chatting with young Miss Clarke when she scanned his books. Her smile always captivated him. Well, he was still youthful, after all. Had a full head of hair, only top dentures, wore contacts mostly, dressed impeccably and drove a Bentley Corniche. Yes, she was single, must be – no wedding nor engagement ring. A boyfriend of her own age? Ridiculous, she was far too intelligent and fancy free to want one of those. No, a settled and financially secure gentleman of leisure, of more mature years, would naturally appeal to her.

Passing through the automatic door he practically collided with someone coming in – a tall, bronze chap wearing a trilby and gabardine mac. The Russian oligarch, who had in fact just ventured into the village to post a letter to an old lady in Mouse Lane.

33

When Miss Parrish eventually returned to her thatched cottage, after visiting Larch Close to return the Geiger counter and power pack to Mr Edwards at his bungalow, she was already formulating a theory of considerable merit regarding the case of the obese man poisoned by an act of nuclear terrorism on the Santa Special.

Stepping off the icy path and into her home, she noticed a single envelope laying on the hairy 'Welcome' mat. She stamped her shoes, removing her coat, mittens and bobble hat, before leaning over to retrieve the letter. No post mark, no stamp – hand delivered by someone other than the postman, then. One of the oligarch's multitudes of secretaries or lackeys, she supposed, maybe even a chauffeur. But she instinctively knew it came from Mr Petrovich.

The Russian would surely have received her own Clintons notelet by now, read it with considerable interest, no doubt.

Waltzing into her sitting room with its low, timbered ceiling and brick chimney piece, she whistled a snatch from Mozart's *Marriage of Figaro* and settled down in her armchair. Ripping open the envelope, she was far from disappointed.

My dear, clever Miss Parrish,
Meet me at the library at noon, we have much to discuss.
Yours,
Oleg

The note was written in Biro, neat and succinct, directly from the man himself. The old lady was much impressed. Already she felt him much more down to earth and practical than many would care to give him credit for. Oh yes, this Russian oligarch was a man she could deal with. She felt certain she was on the brink of solving a most cleverly orchestrated and perfectly executed crime of murder. A railway crime, to be sure, but one that would match the great crimes of history for its ingenuity.

34

Brigadier Eames blundered into the library, glanced briefly at the counter and left in a huff. Still no sign of his adorable junior librarian, the pretty blonde was nowhere to be seen. Possibly at lunch. Ah well, try another day. He chanced upon the figure of Miss Parrish huddled over by the computer section, talking in hushed tones to somebody. But it was Miss Clarke who held sway with his heart and he did not linger, but headed back out into the freezing cold. The automatic door clicked behind him and he was gone.

'Yelena and Svetlana are your daughters, are they not?' said the old lady softly, keeping her voice low.

The handsome, bronzed man in his early sixties before her broke into a troubled grimace. A solid gold Rolex twinkled under the fluorescent glare of the library sanctum.

'They are. My girls are very talented musicians and live much of the year in Moscow and attend the Conservatoire. You will no doubt have seen the concert on television where Yelena won fourth prize.'

'Just so, and it was they who introduced the thallium into the mince pie that eventually killed your compatriot on the Santa Special. I am opting for thallium over polonium, which would of course be impossible to pick up on a small Geiger counter such as the one I borrowed from Mr Edwards.'

'Polonium was not the poison ingested into Andraev

Ivanovich's stomach, but I would be inclined to discount thallium also. You are close. Let's leave it at that for now.'

'Was that Russian Ivanovich a business rival, a competitor to your vast empire? Someone who, shall we put it crudely, needed eliminating?'

'My dear, clever Miss Parrish, I would not be sitting here in this most delightful of rural English country libraries talking to you over a computer desk if that were the case. Oh, I have become a library member, by the way.' He beamed, his features creasing into a boyish grin that made the years fall away. 'You see, this naughty fellow Ivanovich was a killer, a member of Moscow's criminal underworld, an assassin responsible for the untimely death of more than a few close friends of mine. The fact that he happened to shoot my wife, Clara, leave her bleeding to death after accidentally mistaking her for someone else outside the exclusive department store GUM in Red Square, was a determining factor, certainly.'

'I'm so, so sorry, Mr Petrovich – I had no idea,' said a shocked Miss Parrish, frowning her displeasure. 'He killed your wife, you say – Yelena and Svetlana's mother?'

'The dirty fiend killed many more besides. Affable, a connoisseur of fine wines and rich food, vodka anise, he was a gun for hire.'

'How depressingly awful for you.'

'Oh, I imagine he would have read the paper or seen the news that same evening on television – all about a woman in furs shot dead outside GUM's – but not cared two figs. He was paid well after all, even if he did "balls it up". Oh, pardon the expression, Miss Parrish, forgive my uncouth "gangster speak" – I loathe crude language, I can assure you.'

'Perfectly all right, Mr Petrovich. So, you would class this overweight, outwardly genial man as Mafia?'

'Undoubtedly, the links are plain to see.'

'But how did you conceive of such an effective plan to lure him to England and presumably join your employ?'

'Simply an enormous sum of money. I advertised for a bodyguard at unbelievably high rates of pay. He applied, I interviewed him at my Moscow office and I gave him a job. The rest was relatively easy, as they say. Yelena and Svetlana naturally wished to avenge their mother's death. We Russians have this knack of conspiring together, you know – against a common enemy, I mean.'

'They are to be congratulated,' said the old lady with feeling, taking out her purse and procuring her ticket stub for the Santa Special excursion. 'And this?'

The trilby-hatted gentleman smiled when he considered the excursion ticket and gave it back.

'We worked it all out, a long time in advance. Mrs Clagg's boarding house was chosen due to her husband's involvement with the preserved railway. You may not be aware of this, but I am myself a popular classic car enthusiast and have a passion for old trains of yesteryear. I recall Andraev Ivanovich shared my interest. We visited that quaint, rural "Steam Open Day" together, where my collection of ZiLs was displayed, but by then I can assure you a foolproof plan was being hatched.'

'Almost foolproof,' chuckled Miss Parrish, gathering her handbag and things together, preparing to leave the library.

'Almost,' the oligarch laughed. 'Until you came on the scene, that is, my dear. Would you accept an invitation to visit Birchpark Estate for Christmas lunch? Yelena and Svetlana will be there. They haven't left the country, of course, but will be practising in the music room back home. I should get back, they'll miss their papa.'

'I should be delighted,' answered Miss Parrish, glancing

over at the counter where the junior librarian seemed to be looking in their direction, a scowl on her normally pretty face. Perhaps they had been talking too loud. She most fervently hoped and prayed not. 'May I bring my nephew Wilberforce and my best friend, Edie Blenchley?' she queried as an afterthought.

'Certainly. I shall arrange to pick you all up in one of my cars,' the friendly Russian mentioned as they walked arm in arm towards the automatic door, all steely eyes in the local library, old and young alike, fixed upon them.

35

The Father Christmas excursions – the Santa Specials, Mince Pie Special and North Pole Express – finally ended on the 23rd of December, and the preserved railway now closed through the winter months to re-open to the public at Easter weekend.

Snow lay deep and thick about the loco shed. The station buildings were frozen with icicles, the tracks, with no trains running, soon filled in, becoming more of a trail than a railway line until that too vanished under a blanket of white. In fact, the whole of Bramley village was, during that memorably cold spell, icebound. Perfect Yuletide weather, provided you had an Aga, central heating turned up full and a roaring fire in the grate.

On Christmas Eve residents made their way precariously to the little squat Saxon church for the annual carol service.

The Claggs, Vera and Stan, were no exception. After a slap-up meal at the new three-star restaurant, which used to be the 'olde Tudor' tea rooms run by the Sparrow twins, they dutifully attended midnight service at the parish church. The Reverend Eaton presided over a traditional festival of carols and candlelit service popular with villagers and well attended each year. Last year the weather had been rain, floods and gales, this year the static, intemperate magnificence of a freezing Arctic winter.

It was at the carol service, then, that the man with the shaved head first made an appearance. Broad shouldered, fit and muscular like a power lifter – a fanatical body-builder – he wore a navy blue sports jacket and jeans and a clumpy pair of ski boots. He had been politely asking, in broken English, the whereabouts of the Birchpark Estate. Did a Mr Petrovich live here in Bramley? Was there a railway? Milling about with parishioners outside the porch he blended in well and seemed a nice enough man, albeit a complete stranger to the locality. Unseasonably bronzed, he had most likely flown in from somewhere abroad, for he spoke with what could best be described as an Eastern European accent. The vicar, the Reverend Eaton, was quick to make him feel welcome, as did other members of the congregation huddled outside the church after the midnight service, preparing to either drive or walk back home. This convivial group included the Claggs.

'His accent is so much like Yelena's and Svetlana's,' Vera Clagg confided to her husband Stan as they trudged arm in arm through the snowy churchyard to the lych gate. 'A Russian – I'm certain of it.'

'Must be someone on the staff of the oligarch, popped down from Birchpark for the service. An acquaintance of Mr Petrovich, I expect.'

But the man with the shaven, square, Teutonic head, heavy lips and broken nose was not an acquaintance of Mr Petrovich. Actually he was an acquaintance of the obese man suddenly taken ill on the Santa Special. They had promised to meet up in Finland – the capital, Helsinki: go out of town for some skiing or fishing for burbot – but his confederate had not turned up and the mobile signal was dead, the personal website vanished also. This was unprecedented. They always kept in touch, met up for a lark at Christmas and the New Year. The last message had come via text – a stupid, jokey message about some

'Santa Special', an old English tradition kept on the railways. SANTA SPECIAL? He planned to find out more...

36

This Christmas was so different ... indeed exceptional. Edie Blenchley had been thoroughly spoiled, she had never experienced anything quite like it.

On Christmas Day itself, Mr Petrovich, the billionaire oligarch, had piloted his own aircraft – that vivid red helicopter, the Bell Executive – flying a party of guests at a powerful rate of knots over the Downs to the coast. The view from that altitude was panoramic. The snowy, frozen landscape, grazing sheep dotted about, villages, farms and rural homesteads seen in miniature with smoking chimney pots, the odd car or matchbox-sized van tearing along the roads from above.

While sat aloft, strapped in her plush seat next to Miss Parrish, Edie felt perfectly at ease during the flight and entirely safe with Mr Petrovich at the controls. It must be said both ladies were overwhelmed by the kindness and obvious care that had been lavished on guests to ensure their Christmas lunch at Birchpark was a memorable one, with Yelena and Svetlana a constant joy, chatting and laughing. The girls were flying back to Moscow for the New Year, but would not be using a commercial flight, an Aeroflot Jumbo or Airbus, but the far more exclusive Gulf Stream private jet owned by their father.

An after-lunch walk with the dogs had taken the ladies to a forested area, a large wood where a brand new gymnasium-sauna complex was under construction, walls of bricks rising from the ground, the foundations of certain areas being recently set with reinforced concrete.

37

A fortnight following Christmas, Brigadier Eames was summoned to the vicarage by the Reverend Eaton to discuss a matter of some urgency.

The vicarage was a modern and pleasant family-sized home and garden that had in the late seventies replaced the gloomy old Victorian pile with all its draughty rooms, outdated lino-clad bathrooms and vast kitchen and basement quarters; fine in an era of a large, below-stairs retinue of servants when a country parson had ten children to clothe and feed, but a colossal waste of space and much too expensive to maintain in the modern era. So large a residence cost a fortune in heating bills and the garden had become overgrown – weedy paths, encroaching ivy and rhododendron bushes at every turn, the old shed and glasshouse and walled vegetable garden in decline, with no head gardener or staff being recruited since the war. Thankfully, when the youthful and enthusiastic Reverend Eaton, a bachelor, had taken up his incumbency, he had a nice modern, centrally-heated place to move into, with an attached garage to house his mountain bike and estate car.

Over a glass of sherry in the sunny living room, the big freeze having relented its grip and a thaw in progress, the garden being kept tidy by a lady from the village, the patio visible from the French window, the gangly clergyman crossed his long legs and proposed action.

'That awful old piano simply has to go, Brigadier. The choirmaster tells me the instrument plays out of tune and that certain of the keys stick, making even the rendition of a simple hymn a nightmare for the pianist. Have we any ideas?'

'Another piano!' The old soldier thought for a moment. 'I suppose they can easily enough be purchased second-hand for two hundred pounds or so.'

'I'm thinking more BRAND NEW PIANO – a furnishing we can display in the church hall with pride, something to be played for generations to come. A quality instrument. Why, oh why, must we always embrace the lowest common denominator when discussing items for the church hall? We don't want any more off-loaded charity shop junk. There is, I believe a reputable music shop in town, "Godfrey's Music", isn't there?'

'I know the place.' The brigadier scowled at his sherry glass so hard it might break into tiny fragments. 'But it's expensive, Vicar, damned expensive.'

'But at least they sell pianos that won't play out of tune, where the keys don't stick.'

38

Piano Appeal by the Bramley Village Arts Committee
Patron Brigadier Eames

We have been discussing for some time the possibility of acquiring a decent piano for the church hall for concerts and so forth. The old upright has frankly had its day and a reputable tuner told us it was un-playable. Therefore, we have decided to raise an appeal for a new one. We thought a good way to contribute funds was to sponsor a piano key, each of you donating, say, a minimum of £15 per key. Donors would have their names associated with a note and we could produce a poster.

It was now mid-March and Miss Parrish had only just planted some bulbs and finished rinsing her hands under the sink tap when there was a loud hammering at the window. It was her best friend and near neighbour Edie Blenchley, who was obviously frantic about something and kept making curious startled faces, her nose squashed against the pane. Miss Parrish turned off the tap and hurried over to open the back door.

'What's the matter, Edie? Now settle down and I'll pour us a nice cup of tea – there's plenty in the pot.'

'Oh, it's so ghastly, Sybil! One of the removal men, you know over at the church hall shifting that old upright piano, well, he lifted up the dusty lid and stuck his hand down the back and discovered a human skeletal finger bone trapped fast, lodged in amongst the rows of felt hammers and piano wires. No wonder it's sounded so off key all these years!'

'Indeed, my dear, it most certainly adds a touch of the macabre to our Christmas concerts. All those years standing up and applauding at the end of, say, an amateur production of Gilbert and Sullivan or a children's panto, and all the while a mouldering bit of skeleton present in the piano's workings.'

39

The tall Pickfords removal lorry had just backed out onto the main road when the two ladies arrived in Edie's Ford Fiesta. She parked her car on the gravel and they got out, to be greeted by the Reverend Eaton.

'Good afternoon, Miss Parrish – and you, Miss Blenchley. I'm just off to wheel Mrs Quinn up the lane to the outpatients clinic at the cottage hospital. She's just having her six monthly check-up – nothing drastic.'

'That's a fair way to push a wheelchair, Vicar. Doesn't she have one of those mobility scooters?'

'Dratted battery's flat, apparently – forgot to plug in to recharge. Mrs Quinn is a bit forgetful. I don't mind – fresh air'll do me good. The new baby grand looks very refined. £1,600 was an absolute bargain. Mr Herbert, our choirmaster, has already played the keyboard and reckons it's perfect, although Mr Webley, the tuner, is due tomorrow morning to set it up properly.'

'What about the human finger bone, Vicar? Did you contact the police?' asked Miss Parrish, seriously.

'Police? Oh, Lord, no. I mean, maybe it's a piece of chicken bone or something. We did have a bit of a panic on earlier when the removal man found the old digit, but Mrs Hardy, the tea lady, wrapped it in a bit of tinfoil and binned it. Police – oh we don't want to worry them, do we? Waste of an officer's time I expect. Got to come out here from town – diverted from more important duties.'

'Forgive me asking, Vicar, but do any of us know where the piano originally came from? The upright, I mean.'

'Dear me, that's got me thinking. Oh, wait a minute – yes, that would have been the Sparrow sisters, who used to run the tea shop – you know, the place that's now a restaurant. I saw Mr Petrovich in there the other day with one of his associates having lunch. He's a member of our library, you know.'

'The Sparrow twins? So they donated the piano?'

'Indeed, Mrs Hardy was telling me it used to stand in their front room for years. It was in quite good condition before they kindly donated the piano to the church hall. Oh, that must have been many years ago now, before my own time as incumbent.'

'The upright's generally been played at pantomimes and sing-songs, hasn't it?' asked the enquiring old lady, taking her friend's arm, for a moment transfixed by a flight of birds weaving and diving in the overcast sky.

'Quite so. As you know, it stood for years over to one side of the stage. The piano always played out of tune, various keys stuck. Of course we did hire a decent grand piano from town for classical recitals and proper concerts. Wouldn't dream of using an old upright for Mozart or Beethoven concertos, would we?'

The Sparrow twins, both of them spry and cheerful in their old age, well able to shop and fend for themselves despite being in their mid eighties – one even had a little Morris car she drove – lived in a very smart bungalow in Larch Close, quite near to the retired physics master, Mr Edwards, in fact. When she returned to her thatched cottage in Mouse Lane, Miss Parrish decided to make discreet enquiries and called the Sparrows on her mobile.

The gist of the cordial conversation that ensued was,

yes, the Sparrow twins had owned the upright for a number of years before donating it to the church hall. It had stood in their drawing room but that, far from buying it for themselves from a music shop in town, the piano had originally come to them second-hand from the old asylum. The ladies had strong ties because long ago one of the sisters had borne a child out of wedlock, an illegitimate girl, the father a nondescript insurance salesman who shunned parental responsibility and who later went abroad. So she never married and, as she was only seventeen at the time, and this was the late Edwardian era, her baby was confiscated. But, when the baby turned out to be mentally impaired with what would now be treated as Down's Syndrome and perfectly acceptable, the child ended up in a ward at the Birchpark asylum and spent the remainder of her life confined to that same old local institution. Naturally, times changed and rules relaxed, the twin sister being occasionally allowed to visit her illegitimate daughter, and hence some time in the 1950s was offered by a friendly charge nurse the upright piano that had stood for many years, mostly unused and unloved, in a corner of the food hall – for five pounds.

40

The snows of winter had cleared, the village recovering from a period of hibernation. The weather was finer, warmer, and more locals were using the resources of their library – the elderly in particular.

Miss Clarke had been scowling at her computer, checking up on fines to be paid, books overdrawn, when she glanced over the heads of a rapidly diminishing queue at the counter and saw a man wearing a navy blue sports jacket loitering over by the crime section. The man was stocky, wide-shouldered, completely bald, middle-aged and bronzed from the sun. He ran his finger along the row of books, until he picked out a P. D. James title. A book Miss Clarke recalled she had re-stocked from the 'IN' trolley, that is, from a stack of recently returned library books, only that same morning before coffee break.

The fellow grunted, replaced the book, turned on his heel and hurriedly came across to the counter. He was served by old Dorothy Simms and was requesting information ... but not about library books.

'Do you know of Oleg Petrovich?' he asked the old lady in a broken, foreign accent.

'I'm sorry – Petrovich? As you can see, we are quite busy. Are you perchance referring to an author? I can look him up on our lists. Travel writer, is he? Now, if you would just give me a minute or two.'

'No, not to worry,' he insisted gruffly, disconcerted by

the way the trainee junior librarian, the pretty, leggy, blonde Miss Clarke was staring at him, for she found him as a person somehow menacing, bogus, not being entirely truthful about his intentions. Why did he want to know about Mr Petrovich? she wondered, recalling the kindly, Russian gentleman who regularly used their library. Why was he hanging about over by the crime section for over half an hour? Because he hoped to confront him, follow him home? Something rankled about him.

'Have you your library card?' she asked rather tersely, interrupting Dorothy, leaning across to talk to him directly whilst brandishing her date stamp like a threatening weapon.

Without further delay, the bald man in the trendy sports jacket hurried away to the automatic door, somehow embarrassed, annoyed to have been asked about a library card as if it was tied up with an identification process, chillingly reminiscent of passport control or matters of state security.

41

Over Christmas lunch at Birchpark, Mr Petrovich had confided that the radioactive body of the deceased former hit man, member of Moscow's criminal underworld, had been deposited in a special lead-lined metal container and shipped direct from the cottage hospital by articulated lorry to his extensive private grounds. It had been carefully vaulted in a massive quantity of reinforced concrete that now formed part of the foundations to an ultra-modern gymnasium and sauna complex being constructed in the nearby woods.

Miss Parrish proposed that, however ingenious was the method of disposing of the body, the odious gangster had been poisoned by a nuclear mince pie on a Santa Special outing and surely at some stage the victim's presence would be missed back home in Russia. Pertinent questions would be asked by his immediate family, for example, or worse … much worse, by his old associates in the Russian Mafia. Had Mr Petrovich considered this point? she wondered. Well, champagne corks popped, lunch and a long walk flowed into a gloriously memorable tea. Who cared? It was Christmas, after all!

But that was then … now was different. When Miss Parrish was last in the library changing her books, the attractive junior librarian, Miss Clarke, happened to mention the presence of a stranger over by the crime section and how he had enquired at the desk about Mr Petrovich. This most decidedly set alarm bells ringing, in the old lady's mind at least, and she arranged to meet the oligarch at noon, usual place. He regularly shopped and walked around the village and was very free and easy about his personal security in Bramley. He hardly ever travelled in a car, preferring to mingle and chat with locals at the Post Office store, practically as though the village was his own personal fiefdom, which of course in some ways, you might say it actually was, for the positive influence of his personal wealth was everywhere.

For example, the little preserved railway had extended to Fenley, where a brand new signal box was being built: an old Victorian Midland line building meticulously dismantled, numbered brick by numbered brick, and transferred by lorry. Bramley Cross station now had a buffet, gift shop and a museum being constructed. Where was the finance coming from?

'This stranger,' she whispered, crouched over the computer's desk top, Oleg Petrovich huddled beside her on a swivel chair, as people browsed about the shelves choosing books. 'Might I sincerely suggest he could mean you harm? He was foreign, after all, perhaps Russian. Mightn't it be prudent to disappear for a while?'

'My dear, clever lady,' the Russian, looking very dapper in his Norwegian roll-neck sweater and ski jacket, said in a low, husky voice, soundly of the opinion that Miss Parrish was letting her imagination run away with her. 'At present, you should not concern yourself too much with this stranger. But I have something of greater interest I wish to discuss with you. That is why I agreed to meet you here at the library.'

'Really – and that is?' she queried, putting on her half-moon gold spectacles, her brightly intelligent eyes alive with curiosity.

'An item of local history.' He nudged a large brown envelope in her direction. 'Yours – keep it – read it at your own leisure, Miss Parrish. Just some photos I took and local Health Authority documents I researched off the web.'

'Does it concern your property – the old Victorian asylum?'

'How perceptive of you. Indeed it does. The forest area, to be precise.'

'Where you, ahem ... concreted a certain metal, lead-lined container.'

'Close by, in fact. One of my men discovered some gnarled old tree trunks, the bark struck long ago by lightning, blackened and hollowed out. We want to lift the roots using a digger, clear the area of bracken and tree stumps. It's going to be a mucky and difficult job, but I tell you plainly, inside a row of three of these lightning-blackened stumps were human remains. Well, I should say skeletal remains. In the first, a human skull, the second a rib-cage, and the third containing bits of fibula and tibia, knee joints, you know, the lower extremities of a body. I photographed the old groups of bones on my digital camera.'

'How absolutely fascinating!'

'Indeed, I wondered if the bones could be medieval, Tudor even, but after a bit of impromptu research I think they're more recent. I'm having some bone fragments analyzed by a private forensic company. You'll never countenance this, my dear lady, but I'm of the strong opinion somebody was murdered!'

'And the body cut up and concealed in the woods. Oh, how utterly gruesome! I must tell my friend Edie Blenchley. You know Edie, who came over to you for Christmas lunch.'

'And your nephew, Wilberforce – how can I forget?' He chuckled, glancing over his shoulder at the quiet, civilized scene. The English public library, a national institution: Miss Clarke becoming ever less visible behind a pile of returned books, helpful staff on hand to check for titles, mostly intelligent folk who shared an unabiding love of fine entertaining literature and books. But the library, dare we say it, is also a place where, if you're not careful, you can easily be overheard.

And they had been – *overheard,* that is. The ever resourceful and enquiring bald-headed man, this time wearing a disguise of thickly lensed glasses and an old lady's wig picked up from a charity shop, was at that moment concealed over by the travel section skulking behind the bookshelves. Intelligence gathering was the official jargon, and so far he had managed to overhear the majority of the conversation taking place between Petrovich and that Parrish woman at the computer desk. He had every reason to feel satisfied – he had learnt enough now to plan ahead.

'An eye for an eye,' he muttered under his breath, startled when he looked up to find that blonde bitch was staring darkly at him, idly tapping her date stamp on the desk. She, a junior librarian for God's sake, who had so rudely demanded to see his identification papers, or rather library card, the last time he was in. He must clear out, get away from the librarian's suspicious, mean stare. 'An eye for an eye,' he said, in Russian this time, heading determinedly for the automatic door.

42

Miss Clarke, after saying goodbye to her librarian colleague and best mate, Tessa Layton, in the leafy forecourt, walked up the road to catch the community bus from the request stop. This service now operated regularly from Bramley, through Brocklehurst village, taking a roundabout rural route into town, the former country-line bus route in fact before it was scrapped.

The bus arrived, Miss Clarke got her ticket and made her way to the rear seats. The Mercedes bus was proving popular and its twin, a motor bus with identical grey and cream coachwork, formed part of the company's fleet, used for day trips to London's theatre land, visiting National Trust properties, days out to the seaside and so forth, booked by phone or online.

The community bus went round by the war memorial and headed for Cottage Hospital Corner, where the new modern maternity wing and outpatients were situated. Miss Clarke sat by the window, languidly staring out at a row of bungalows, prim gardens emerging from winter. When the vehicle drove into a lay-by and stopped to offload passengers, she noticed across the road there was an allotment. Then her eyes widened in surprise, she pressed her face close up to the bus window, wiping away some condensation with her glove ... it was him ... The baldy who she had seen acting suspiciously in the library, the body-builder type with the shaved head. She watched fascinated as he emerged from a shack, a garden shed with a rolled asphalt roof, wearing an Iron Maiden T-shirt tucked into his jeans that showed off his taut biceps and dragon tattoos. The junior librarian got the distinct impression he was lying low, using the shed as make-do accommodation and a hide-out for the last month or so.

As the community bus pulled away, she turned and glanced back just in time to see him snatch a gold-plated mobile phone from his back pocket and punch in some numbers.

43

Miss Parrish took a sip from her glass of elderflower wine, while she sat on the sofa next to her best friend Edie Blenchley, the two ladies closeted most agreeably for a chilly March evening in the sitting room of her comfortable thatched cottage in Mouse Lane. Apart from their shrill gossipy voices, the only sound was the familiar buzzing filaments on the electric coal fire aglow in the chimney piece, a brass vase of dried corn stacks and wild flowers displayed prettily in the hearth.

It would perhaps be expected that talk centred on such homely topics as knitting patterns, cacti, or the latest coming events over at the church hall put on by the Bramley Arts Committee. In fact they were discussing murder. Skeletal remains to be more precise! Fanned-out colour snaps littered the glass top of the coffee table.

'You mean to say, the finger bone found in the old upright piano by the Pickfords removal man, and the bits of a skeleton found in the tree stumps, could be linked? Is that what you're saying, Sybil?'

'Oh yes, what we are dealing with here is a body dismembered up at the old asylum – all old bones now, of course, the remains discovered quite randomly. The idea, you see, was to uproot the ancient stumps using a digger, level the ground for landscaping. I see your glass is empty, Edie. May I offer you something stronger? Sanatogen tonic wine, perhaps?'

'Elderflower is fine, thank you, Sybil. I will have another half glass, if you please.'

'And you will recall me telling you that the old upright, although donated to the church hall by the Sparrow twins, originally came from the asylum. One of the ladies purchased it for five pounds from a charge nurse. Now that's a bit odd, isn't it? I mean, you would expect a bursar or administrator to be dealing with the sale of items, property belonging to the Health Authority, wouldn't you?'

'Well, a nurse on a ward might have been delegated such a task.'

'Oh, in those days I should imagine there was a very strict pecking order on the administration side. A charge nurse, a professional carer, selling ward furniture – no, I don't think that likely.'

Miss Parrish poured out some more wine and handed Edie Blenchley a glass before resuming her seat on the sofa. She replaced her half-moon spectacles and sifted through the various photographs taken on Mr Petrovich's digital camera.

'The lightning-damaged, hollowed-out stumps were a perfect hiding place, deep in the dark, deciduous woods where few people ventured. The body of the victim first cut up into three pieces, perhaps in the bath-house at the asylum, the various segments, the head, the torso and lower extremities each deposited separately. As Mr Petrovich jokingly suggested at our last meeting at the library – "we have, it seems, our very own trunk murder". Of course, we do not know as yet when the actual murder was carried out. It could have been more recent. Forensics will have to decide.'

'And you're to meet the oligarch and go to the woods.'

'Tomorrow morning. I shall take the community bus. There's a stop off for Birchpark Lane.'

'You have quite a reputation for solving puzzles, Sybil. Have you come up with any theories regarding this old skeleton murder?'

'Why, of course, my dear. One only has to consider the old upright piano. How well they are made to last, the lid closing snugly over the keyboard.'

'The lid?'

'It was slammed down, my dear, slammed so very, very hard in anger. A fit of uncontrollable rage all because a mentally impaired patient was amusing him or herself playing a discordant, jumbled tune over and over again, getting on the staff nurse's nerves. Possibly the patient would play alone in the food hall of an evening. "Stop it – stop that noise!" I can almost hear the carer say. Murder and dismemberment in the bath-house followed. I cannot be certain, of course, but that is my belief.'

'How vividly you put these things, Sybil, but it does make sound sense – the lid being slammed down on a pair of fragile hands, a finger shorn off and hurriedly deposited by the angry charge nurse down the back of the piano – how perfectly horrid.'

44

The bright and gleaming community bus was running to schedule. The bald, stocky man with a red face, a habitué of the gym and weights and power lifting, wore a maroon ski jacket, jeans and an open-necked denim shirt. He sat by the centre aisle, morosely considering the passing scene through the windows, the monotonous stretches of dual carriageway interspersed by the occasional roundabout, the fast-moving traffic shooting past. A big, grey and imposing speed camera box supported on a metal pole to the grassy verge and a parked traffic police 4x4 in distinctive blue and yellow Battenberg livery caught his attention. Lights and strobes started flashing and it zoomed past. 'After a speeding biker,' he thought grimly.

The trouble was he felt incredibly tense, not loose and amiable, nonchalant even, as he should when carrying out a mission. The problem was that old lady in the third row who kept staring at him. The formidable old woman sat knitting from balls of wool in her leather shopping bag was Miss Parrish, that damned confidante of Petrovich's – the man he was sworn to kill. She had boarded the bus at the war memorial sporting her bag, brolly, M&S coat and hat and a pair of sensibly stout walking shoes. She had a dotty, scatterbrained demeanour common to elderly spinsters in an English country village, he supposed, but there was a steely, almost contemptuous gaze that surfaced occasionally, which he found unnerving. Knitting

113

was not the only thing on her mind, he rightly deduced.

The community bus drew into the next request stop along the verge. Miss Parrish stepped off the bus and took a brisk walk up the lane – the turn-off from the dual carriageway. Mr Petrovich had agreed to meet her near his home. He had mentioned the time and place quite loudly in the library the other day. The friendly beep of a horn soon announced his arrival, Mr Petrovich driving an open-top Mini Moke, a little runabout popular in the sixties.

Together, in an unhurried, chatty way, after opening a five-barred gate the friends headed up the forest trail until they reached a clearing. Glimpsed through a circle of beech, elder and horse chestnut could be seen the beginnings of the new gymnasium and sauna complex presently under construction. It did not take Miss Parrish long to locate the three hollowed-out tree stumps. Blackened bark from a heat strike by lightning during a severe storm, mushrooms, toadstools and spongy spores of fungal growth grew round the base of each. The area was damp and squidgy underfoot from accumulated layers of rotten leaves. Twigs snapped. Miss Parrish glanced round briefly and gave her trusty brolly a squeeze, smiling to herself all the while. They were not alone…

'Well, Mr Petrovich, I think we do have a local history murder mystery on our hands. My view is, as you know, that we should follow the proper procedure and contact Mr Prior, the curator of our local history museum over at Brocklehurst.'

'Yes, I'll go with that. I found out on the web that they are the county's main repository for papers and memorabilia documenting the lives of inmates and times of the old asylum. I must say that when workmen were gutting and renovating the main building we found nothing of historical interest except a number of old iron bedsteads and institutional potties, the wards and rooms stripped bare. It was only this landscaping job that uncovered a treasure trove of old bones.'

'Quite, we might even attempt a jointly written pamphlet outlining the discovery of an old murder mystery, putting forward our theories as to the likely victim and so forth. The upright piano of course plays its part.'

'Well, we have our forensic pathology. The bones are being carbon dated, which will help decide the era the murder took place in, then we can get started on the documents, maybe even consult some helpful books Miss Clarke could sort out for us.'

The pair chatted away, oblivious to the fact they were being watched by an armed and extremely ruthless gunman. With their shared love of crime fiction they had just got round to discussing the merits of P. D. James over, say, Dorothy Sayers or Dostoevsky, when a catch clicked.

'I've got you, you bastard,' exclaimed someone creeping up behind. 'That filthy, low-down trick of the mince pie on the Santa Special – you've got it coming, Petrovich.'

'I think not,' said Miss Parrish, deftly wielding her pretty, flower-printed Laura Ashley brolly, calmly pointing the colourful umbrella's razor-sharp tip perilously close to the taut muscles of the man's neck. 'You may recall the name Marcov – does it ring a bell? Does it sound familiar? There was a very clever murder committed in London along the embankment a long time ago now by an unknown assassin. Something to do with a banker from Rome, was it not – and a poisoned umbrella!'

'You low-down bitch,' he spat the words out, his ugly, fat face revealing that he was reeling from shock.

'Drop your pistol. One tiny scratch from this brolly, which incidentally I dipped in rat poison earlier – a foul, rusting can of the stuff kept in my potting shed at home, filthy and bacterially infected with grime – and you, my dear, will be facing a painful death. Acute blood poisoning, you see. Nasty rat poison. Oh, you're strong and healthy, so I'd give you a minute or two before the swelling begins, the burning in the throat. Why, my acquaintance Mr Petrovich might even choose to bury you alive in a coma so you can join your odious confederate, the Muscovite hit man, in a similar sealed metal container!'

'It's outrageous!' The bald man screamed for all his great physical prowess and muscular physique, unable to move a neck muscle because of the deadly proximity of the old lady's poisoned brolly. But, preferring life over rat poisoning any day, he dropped his Glock pistol so that the Russian oligarch could easily retrieve it out of harm's way. 'Petrovich, this is too astounding for words. It's patently unfair – humiliating!'

'Then I trust, given a chance, you will leave the country at the earliest opportunity. My Gulf Stream jet will fly you across to Finland, money no object.'

'All right, all right, you canny devil, Petrovich. You and this old woman – you win. Half a million to call the dogs off.'

'Done.'

*   *   *

For the next couple of days, apart from tidying up the garden and planting and hoeing, Sybil Parrish was wholly concerned with matters relating to the local history project she was sharing with Mr Petrovich, pulling together the information she had gleaned from her research earlier in the week. While her Russian friend diligently scanned data on his computer, the old lady herself had paid visits to both her local library in Dean Crescent, plus the main library in the centre of town. She spent her mornings ensconced at her desk in the sitting room at her cottage in Mouse Lane, researching this queer business of the 'old bones' mystery. The pile of books in front of her were, for the most part, long out of print with faded dust jackets, titles of local history interest, the most relevant being *My Parish*, a well-written tome by Amy Lambhurst from the 1950s; likewise *Branch Line Heaven – a Southern Region Gem* by Colonel C. Brinkley, and *Church and Parish – a Memoir* by the Reverend Atkins MA (Oxon). All these non-fiction titles had one thing in common – each mentioned the old asylum at Birchpark in a similar context.

'My own recollections for that Sunday are quite distinct, for I recall, apart from the May Day Fair, me making jams and so on, the vicar at our church made special mention at his pulpit address that we should all be especially vigilant for an inmate had escaped from the asylum on the hill, although we never were properly informed as to whether this escapee was dangerous or not. A description was given but it was really so vague as to be useless. We heard the police whistles and tracker dogs that night but it soon died down. I recall one old dear, well over ninety, who had lived at that old tithe cottage belonging to the manor on the corner most of her life, calling me over and saying in a croaky voice, 'Allus maybe we'se get us froats slit fro' ear to ear if you'rn forgotten ta close ye winda o' a nighttime girlie', which put the wind up me something rotten, I can tell you.'

'Our local branch, some might recall, in the 1950s became part of a county-wide police investigation when it was discovered a resident of the asylum had managed to escape and was on the run. Had he purchased tickets for London from our local station? Had a stranger been seen loitering on the platform or in the station waiting room? Had he perchance walked along the tracks, avoiding main thoroughfares and public scrutiny? Passengers at Bramley were questioned by police by way of an enquiry for a week or so – but nothing came of it.'

'Bramley and Brocklehurst are by far my favourite parishes. My incumbency lasted until retirement, and as the local vicar for many years at our beautiful, old Saxon church, I oversaw both happy and sad events in our village. Do you remember the death of our beloved squire, old Jordan Croft? The endlessly long funeral procession that began at the manor and passed through our village? What a prestigious event. I can see it now, the squire's oaken coffin borne upon a century-old farm wagon, that old Rolls Royce Phantom II of his taking up the rear, covered in floral tributes and wreaths, men folk removing their hats in memory of he who had once owned the lands and estates hereabouts. The high street, shuttered, every curtain drawn along the route. Such solemnity and respect, and then, out of nowhere, police whistles, police cars tearing past the funeral cortege, bells clanging – disgraceful, all that row! And what for, I ask you? Some inmate had apparently escaped from that asylum and good luck to him, I say. They never did catch the blighter, did they? Got clean away!'

But the inmate had never escaped in the first place, nor

even strayed from the precincts of the asylum, decided Miss Parrish, removing her half-moon spectacles and placing the book with its marker carefully with the others on her desk. Why? Because the man was already dead, *murdered* – the body parts transferred to the woods by the charge nurse. The hospital alert was a clever ruse to deflect suspicion – to explain away why a patient should have suddenly gone absent from the ward.

The mobile phone lit up and trembled. There was the ding-dang-dong tune of the ring tone. It was not Edie Blenchley, as she had expected, but Mr Petrovich and he sounded excited.

'The carbon dating, Miss Parrish,' he said breathlessly. 'It's come through at last. The forensic lab sent me the data.'

'1950s,' she answered calmly. 'More recent than our own estimate.'

'Why yes, that's absolutely spot on. But how – how did you know?'

'I think I might have a better idea of who those old bones actually belonged to now.'

She sipped the dregs of her milky coffee thoughtfully, watching the sparrows fluttering their wings, bathing in the bowl of the granite bird bath at the centre of her lawn, amazed how a carer, this charge nurse, could get away with murder.

'A charge nurse, you say?' spluttered the oligarch. 'I wonder, Miss Parrish, would you like to visit Finland tomorrow? My Gulf Stream jet will leave at 10a.m. We are, of course, transferring Mr Rosonov back to Helsinki. There's a little matter of some cash I need to hand over to his business associates, which shouldn't divert too much of our time, then we could push on to visit Ainola, Sibelius' home at Järvenpää.'

'Well, as you know, Mr Petrovich, I do so like classical music. I have a CD of "Finlandia" of course. Might Miss Blenchley come along for the ride also?'

'Why certainly. Just leave your passports with my secretary when she calls later. I shall personally arrange for all the formalities to be sorted out.'

'The aircraft will take off from where?'

'Felchester aerodrome.'

'Is that Felchester Gliding Club?'

'There are gliders, mostly helicopters and a few privately operated jets kept hangared there. My Gulf Stream can take off and land on very short runways, incidentally.'

After Mr Petrovich's call, Miss Parrish went and poured herself a glass of Sanatogen tonic wine. This flyaway day had taken her quite by surprise. After all, she was more used to booking up for a coach trip in town, although she had travelled over to Paris on the Eurostar with Edie once.

45

The following morning, at ten o'clock precisely, Miss Parrish and Edie Blenchley found themselves taking to the skies. The Gulf Stream jet trundled along the tarmac runway at Felchester aerodrome, past the parked gliders and the odd helicopter, the wind sock busily blowing sou'-easterly, and, with a tremendous surge of power and increased whine and thrust of jet engines, the aircraft left the ground and banked steeply into the clouds before levelling out, coordinates set east and on automatic pilot for the duration. Through the cabin window Miss Parrish watched the rapidly diminishing aerodrome and, far below, landmarks such as Bramley's Saxon church became an insignificant dot.

'Well, that *was* exciting!' said Miss Blenchley, still feeling wobbly, her hearing for a time muffled then returning to normal.

Seat belts released, coffee was served and everyone on board the flight to Helsinki settled down to chat and relax. Everyone except the man with the shaven head, now known as Mr Rosonov, who was seated very near the exit door – *conveniently so*. He appeared grim and overly pensive, not finding the trip a pleasurable experience at all. It seemed too good to be true. On the face of it he was being offered a free flight to Finland and half a million sterling – in cash, too. He had been satisfied and shaken hands with Petrovich – a done deal – but for starters, why was he purposely placed back here, away from the other passengers.

A pair of burly fellows interrupted his thoughts. The chef Anton and his hulking, muscle-bound assistant had come out from the ultra modern kitchenette to make an appearance. One of them reached up for the partition curtain and discreetly drew it across the aisle and grinned. The Gulf Stream was presently flying fairly low and out to sea – course set for Scandinavia.

'But where, oh where is Mr Rosonov?' enquired a flustered Miss Parrish, buttoning her M&S coat, looking about her as they approached Customs at Helsinki Airport. 'Is he gone to the loo, I wonder? I'm certain he was seated to the left of the exit door and when I turned round to wave, you know on our approach, he wasn't in his seat.'

'Oh, don't fuss so my dear, clever lady,' laughed Mr Petrovich, helping Miss Parrish with her bag, nudging her forward and smiling at the officials warmly. 'My staff will look after him – I'm sure he's somewhere *or other*. Miss Blenchley, over here if you please. Don't forget we have a car waiting.'